SummerTime

(A Novella)

Adrienne Thompson

Pink Cashmere Publishing

Arkansas, USA

Printed in the United States of America

First Printing 2015

Copyright © 2015 Adrienne Thompson

ISBN: 0-9971461-0-9

ISBN-13: 978-0-9971461-0-3

Heavenly Father, thank You from the bottom of my heart for the trials of my life, for without them, I may never have sought Your face. I love You and I thank You for just being God.

I'd like to extend a special thank you to Sharon Blount and the Building Relationships Around Books Online Book Club, The Sista Girl Book Club, The Page Turners Book Club of Pine Bluff, Arkansas, the Little Rock Alumnae Chapter of Delta Sigma Theta Sorority, Inc., Garbo Hearne and Pyramid Art, Books, & Custom Framing, Sormag's E-reader Book Club, Shalanna Wilhelmsen and the Vanna Heights Book Club, A Place For Books Book Club, the Sexy Book Worms Book Club of NYC, the Between the Pages Book Club of Cincinnati, Ohio, the FB Page Turners, Orsayor Simmons and the Book Referees, OOSA Bookclub, Carl Rykard, Barbara Joe Williams, Arlisha Myrie, Shan Mahogany, Anne Dina Pierre, Sharyn Gray, Tina Brown, Janice Ross, Selena Haskins, Lynette Shelton, Karen Epps Weston, Deborah Dunson, Shanell Banks, Tivona Elliott-Clark, Parker J. Cole, Jeanette SapphireJblue Best Charrette, Angelia Vernon Menchan, Cathy Jo G, Nicole Sharon, LaToya Murchison, Julia Witherspoon, Margie Nesby, Cassondra Wynn, Aja Graves, Tonja Tate, Jessica Garrett, Lareeta Robinson, and Barbara Morgan. If I have omitted anyone's name, please know that I appreciate you and thank God for your support!!

"...I found the one my heart loves..."
Song of Solomon 3:4 NIV

Soundtrack:

"Summertime" Ella Fitzgerald

"Night and Day" Frank Sinatra

"You and the Night and the Music" Frank Sinatra

"Stormy Weather" Lena Horne

"What a Difference a Day Made" Dinah Washington

"New Orleans" Hoagy Carmichael

"Jive at Five" Count Basie

"After Hours" Dizzy Gillespie, Sonny Rollins, and Sonny Stitt

"Round Midnight" Thelonious Monk

"Jump, Jive an' Wail" Louis Prima

"Fools Rush In" Frank Sinatra

"Hot House" Dizzy Gillespie and Charlie Parker

"S' Wonderful" Shirley Bassey

"My Heart Stood Still" Ella Fitzgerald

"The Man I Love" Billie Holiday

Soundtrack Continued:

"Blue Moon" Frank Sinatra

"Good Morning Heartache" Ella Fitzgerald

"They Can't Take That Away From Me" Ella Fitzgerald

"Love Walked In" Louis Armstrong

CHAPTER ONE

"Summertime"

I ran and ran and ran. I ran past the cars, the buildings, the street lights, and the people. I ran until I reached the bridge, then I quickened my steps. I ran across the Arkansas River. I closed my eyes and felt the wind on my face. I felt the burning in my calves. I felt my heart race. But I still ran. I felt the beads of sweat as they began to form on my forehead.

I opened my eyes, sensing that I was nearing the end of the bridge, veered to the right, and continued to run. Having crossed the barrier that separated Little Rock from North Little Rock, I continued to run. I ran until I felt I would collapse, and then I ran even harder. That was what I'd done my entire life. I worked and worked at something until I thought I hit a wall and then I broke through that wall. That was the only way I knew how to operate. It was the only way I knew how to survive.

I ran over the Main Street Bridge, heading back towards my aunt's house-cum-restaurant. I ran the same route at the same time every morning. You could set your watch by it. Consistency is the only way to persevere, that was my motto. I was focused. I had goals to attain. I had to be in shape for that. So I ran.

I slowed my pace for the last leg of my journey, placing my hands on my hips and panting for air as I walked up the steep hill that led to Aunt Iris's house. As if it sensed I was close to home, my body began to relax and it became harder and harder for me to walk up the hill. Finally, the pale yellow house came into view. The worn wooden sign hanging from the front porch read "Loma's Soul Food". Loma was my grandmother, Aunt Iris's mother. She was also my mother's mother. I stopped at the bottom step and caught my breath.

I walked inside and snaked my way through the three huge rooms on the first floor. Once a dining room, living room, and parlor, the rooms were now crammed full of tables and chairs. The first floor had served as a restaurant for more than twenty years, first helmed by Grandma Loma, then by Aunt Iris. I walked slowly up the steep stairs to my bedroom, stretched my sweaty body across the bed, and closed my eyes. Another hour and I'd be downstairs serving breakfast.

I rolled over and smiled at the picture of my mama that sat on the dresser. I sighed. She had so many dreams for me. There was so much I was supposed to do. I was trying, but things just weren't working out the way I'd planned. I closed my eyes again and soon fell asleep.

"Good morning. Welcome to Loma's. My name is J'Nay and

I'll be your server. Are you ready to order?" I delivered my spiel in my sweetest voice and watched as the heavy-set man frowned. His companion, a petite woman, continued to read the menu. Neither of them acknowledged my presence. Being a waitress taught me a lot about people. People could be friendly, gracious, and very kind. On the other hand, people could be cold, detached, and ungrateful. These two were just plain rude.

They continued to study the menu in silence. I stood there trying to ignore the fact that they hadn't acknowledged my presence, pretending that it didn't bother me. But of course, it did. People were like that, though. Sometimes it seemed like people were just so insensitive. Just because I was wearing an apron and a name tag didn't make me any less human than them. Who did they think they were? One day, when I became a famous singer, they'd regret ignoring me. I imagined this same couple approaching me after a concert, asking for my autograph. I imagined my bodyguard, who'd have some name like "Red" or "Big Lou" stopping them in their tracks. "Ms. Walker is not signing autographs right now."

I smiled at the thought.

"I'll have the country omelet minus the bell peppers and an orange juice," the man finally said.

I jotted down the order and turned my attention to the woman.

"Um, I'll have the bacon and egg special," she said.

"How'd you like the eggs?

"Scrambled, hard."

"Toast or biscuit?"

"Biscuit."

"Beverage?"

"Apple juice, oh and black coffee."

I nodded, took their menus, and headed to the kitchen.

I placed the ticket on the counter. The cook, John Folks, smiled at me just like he always did. I smiled back. I knew he was sweet on me. He was kind of shy, but he was always smiling at me, flashing those dimples of his. Always telling me how nice I looked and from time to time, he'd ask me how my music was coming along, though he'd never heard me sing. He was cute, but he wasn't my type. Honestly, no one was my type. I didn't have time for that.

I turned to leave and then remembered I needed a stack of pancakes for table six. When I turned back around, John was grinning from ear to ear, holding a plate of pancakes.

"Um, thank you," I said as I took the plate from him.

He adjusted his round, wire-framed eyeglasses and nodded. "You're welcome," he said softly.

So went the day, order after order, customer after customer. I worked and daydreamed and counted the hours, minutes, and seconds until my shift ended. Afterwards, I'd head to the job I loved. Job number two.

Three o'clock arrived, *finally,* and I headed to the kitchen and ran into my cousin, Linda, who'd work my tables from three until the restaurant closed at 11:00P.M. Linda was twenty and was in her second year of college. Her room was across the hall from mine.

"Slow day for tips," I said. "Hope the evening shift is better for you."

Linda shrugged. "Can't ever tell around here. See you later."

I glanced over at John Folks who was staring at me with those big round eyes of his. Sometimes it felt like he looked right through to my soul and it made me a little uncomfortable. He dropped his gaze when our eyes met. I headed upstairs and took a nap. I had to be at the studio by six.

CHAPTER TWO

"Night and Day"

I parked my car, ran my hand over my afro, checked my face in the mirror, and shook my head at seeing my tired eyes. Climbing out of my old green Toyota, I slung my purse over my shoulder, walked around to the back of the Dab Productions building, and knocked on the rusted metal door. I glanced around me. I hated taking the back entrance. Little Rock wasn't the most dangerous place to live, but it wasn't the safest either. I tapped my foot nervously as I waited. Finally, Dab answered the door.

"What's up, Ms. Holiday?" he greeted me with a wide smile. "Ms. Holiday" was his little nickname for me. He said I had Billie Holiday's vibe.

I smiled. "Hey, Dab." Dab Williams was a local producer mostly known for the parties he threw throughout the city. He made a good living with the parties and other social events that held his name. A couple of years ago he'd rented this building downtown and set up a recording studio. I'd been working for him ever since I answered his ad in the paper for back-up singers. He'd originally hired four of us. I was the only one still working with him.

I'd sung back-up for a couple of R&B acts he was working

with, but for the most part, I'd been singing hooks for rap artists. I didn't particularly like rap, but a girl had to start somewhere, right? In exchange for my services, Dab paid me a decent wage and allowed me a couple hours' studio time every week to work on a demo.

I followed him to his office and sat across from his desk. "What we working on today, Dab?"

Dab, who was tall and wide, settled into his seat with a grunt and propped his feet on his desk. "I need to talk to you."

I nodded. "Okay."

"You know you my girl, right?"

I nodded again. "Yeah, and you my boy. You're letting me live my dream, little by little."

"I sold that song you worked on with the Southwest Mob to Beast Mode records. They want to distribute it."

I sat up straight in my chair. "Wow, Dab! That's great! So we're gonna record it professionally? Not that you're not professional. You know what I mean." I was so excited, I was talking all over myself.

"Uh, that's what I needed to talk to you about. They really dug the song, but they thought your voice was wrong for it. They want another singer to do the hook."

"What?"

"They weren't feeling your style. They said you sounded too polished, too jazzy. Not raw enough for the song."

I stood from the chair. "It's a song about money and rims, Dab. How raw is that?"

He nodded. "I know. I hear you, but this could put these guys on the map. I had to agree to the company's terms."

I blinked back tears. All this time I'd worked so hard and when the break came, I was left out of it. "Too polished? Too jazzy? I'm being punished because I sing too well?"

"Basically, yeah. Look, I'm sorry, Nay. I still wanna work with you. As a matter of fact, why don't you work on your demo tonight? You can stay as long as you want to. Chuck'll help you." Chuck was his engineer-in-training. Chuck was a nice guy but I was upset and there was no telling how I'd treat Chuck if I stayed.

I clutched my purse strap tightly and shook my head. "That's okay. I think I'ma go now." I turned to leave.

Dab stood from his chair. "I fought for you, Nay. I really did. I'm sorry. We get our feet in the door good and I know they'll let me use whoever I want. Just hold on."

I nodded, blinked back more tears, and headed out of his building. Once inside my car, I let loose. I cried and cried. I thought about all the dreams I had. The dreams me and my mom used to discuss. I missed my mom, so I cried harder. Once my tears had subsided, I started my car and drove with no destination in mind.

I finally ended up at Riverfront Park. It was still light out and there were other people there enjoying the late July weather. Couples, some with kids, some without. I'd never had time for that stuff. I'd dated a little but nothing serious. I was always into myself, my future. In high school I spent all of my time rehearsing with my little singing group. In college, I was too busy studying. I was a business major. I figured I needed to know business since I was going to be a star. I dropped out of college after a semester, when I figured I'd learned enough, and went back home to New Orleans. Eventually, Hurricane Katrina had taken my mother from me and led me here to my aunt's house. Here in Little Rock, I was too busy pursuing my career to date. And besides, from what I could tell, dating brought a person little more than heartache and wasted time, neither of which I needed in my life.

I stared out at the water and sighed. Hurricane Katrina had taken my life from me. Back there, I'd had a regular gig singing at a local bar and I'd had my mama, Jessie. I missed her so much. I never knew my father, so my mama was my world. When I was much younger, my grandmother was a huge part of my world, too. My mama and my grandmother, Loma, had molded me. They'd taught me everything I knew. It was from my grandmother that I'd inherited my voice and my love for jazz. She'd babysit me when my mama had to work and she'd play Billie Holiday and Sarah Vaughan records and we'd sing along about Lola getting what she wants or God blessing the child that's got his own. She'd bake peach cobblers for her restaurant and let me be the taste-tester. Oh how I loved her peach cobbler! She'd shell peas and pick greens on my mama's porch. She'd always give me a little bowl of my own so I could help. She'd tell me stories about running her own boarding house and jazz club and about all of the musicians and other people she met. I loved my grandmother.

Then, when I was eight, she moved to Arkansas and she took her restaurant and her music and her memories with her. After that, it was just me and Mama, two peas in a pod. Mama always told me I'd be a star. She said I was destined for greatness. She believed in me. She was my biggest fan, but now she was gone.

I wiped the tears that trickled down my cheek. The day the hurricane hit, I was out of town. I was travelling with a local band, singing backup. When I saw the news on TV, I called Mama and told her to get to higher ground. She said she would after she gathered some things first. I hung up believing that she'd be fine. There'd been hurricane threats before. No one could've foreseen the devastation caused by Katrina. My mama died in that house, my childhood home. She waited too late and the water rose too fast for her and she died. They found her on the second floor.

Mama was why I worked so hard. She believed in me. She

said I was destined for greatness. I *had* to succeed, for her. I *couldn't* fail. I'd be thirty years old in a couple of months. I always thought I'd be a star by thirty. I still had time, though. I knew that. I just had to make it happen. Tomorrow, I'd head back into that studio and finish that demo. I was determined to have my record deal by my thirtieth birthday. I was determined to stand onstage with a spotlight shining on me as I faced a crowd of adoring fans. *It's gonna happen. It's my destiny. I will be a star!*

CHAPTER THREE

"You and the Night and the Music"

I made it home around midnight, and the lights were still on in the restaurant. So I figured my cousins and the rest of the crew were still cleaning up. As I walked in, I heard the most heavenly sounding music. Someone was playing my grandmother's old piano which sat in the corner of the dining room. I walked slowly into the room and saw that it was John Folks. He was playing an old jazzy-sounding piece. I leaned against the door facing and continued to listen. After the news I'd just received, hearing that music soothed me. I closed my eyes and imagined myself singing to it.

The music abruptly stopped and I opened my eyes. John was looking up at me, wearing a look of embarrassment on his face. "I didn't know you were here," he said softly.

"I just made it back. I didn't know you were a musician." I didn't know much about John Folks. I guess I'd never tried to find out.

He nodded. His ruddy-colored skin seemed even redder, as if he was blushing. "Yeah, I majored in music in college."

I moved closer to him. "Really? You went to college?"

"Yeah, but I didn't finish. That's why I'm working here. I'm trying to save up to go back." I think that was the most I'd

ever heard John Folks talk at one time in the year or so he'd
worked at my aunt's restaurant.

"That's great, John."

"Yeah."

"Will you play some more?"

He smiled and nodded.

I sat down next to him on the bench, closed my eyes, and
listened as his long fingers stroked the keys on the piano like a
trained professional. This time, he played a song that I
recognized, an old jazz standard—"Summertime." I began to
hum along. I opened my eyes and John was staring at me as he
continued to play. I smiled at him.

"That was one of my Grandma Loma's favorites."

He returned my smile. "It's one of my favorites, too. You
have a really nice voice, J'Nay."

"Thanks, John."

We sat there humming and playing and it felt nice. At that
moment, I felt like I'd known John Folks all my life. The
music had connected us in a way I can't explain. So much so
that I didn't want the moment to end. When my aunt walked
into the room and announced that she was going to cut the
lights off, I felt a little disappointed.

"Well, good night, John. Hey, you should play more often.
You're really good."

"Thanks, but Ms. Iris doesn't pay me to play piano."

I smiled. "I hear you. Well, see you in the morning."

"Yeah, good night."

I stood to leave and John stood beside me. His tall, thin frame towered over me. "Um, can I ask you something, J'Nay?" he said softly, his eyes piercing mine.

I nodded. "Sure. What is it?"

He moved a little closer, his eyes still locked on mine. "Do you think that maybe we could go out sometime? Maybe for dinner or a movie or something?"

"Um, I don't know, John. I'm pretty busy here and at my second job, and I don't really date."

He dropped his eyes. "Oh, okay. Well, see you later, then."

"See you later."

As I walked up the stairs, I thought about John. He was sweet and all, but I was on a mission, and I wasn't about to let anything or anyone take my focus.

Chapter Four

"Stormy Weather"

Some days you know from the time you wake up that it's not going to be a good day. This was one of those days. I woke up with a slight headache, and although a couple of aspirin fixed the pain, I still felt off-balance for the remainder of the morning. It was raining cats and dogs and rain always brought the crazies into the restaurant. People would come in and order as little as a cup of coffee and sit for hours just to avoid the rain. I don't have to tell you what that does to a waitress's tips.

Aunt Iris wasn't feeling well. For most people that would mean that they'd skip work for the day. Not Aunt Iris. She reported to work as usual, but had an attitude the size of Texas all morning long. Aunt Iris's son, Ronnie, was working the morning shift with me that day. He was usually good for a laugh or two with his dry wit, but with his mother on the war path, he stayed pretty quiet.

On top of everything else, John Folks had called in sick that morning, so the kitchen staff was short. I half-wondered if he was so upset about me turning him down that he'd skipped out on work, then I told myself that was a silly notion. It wasn't like he was in love with me or anything. I have to admit one thing, though; I kind of missed seeing him and his smile. I really could've used one of his smiles that morning.

It was near the end of my shift that morning when my headache returned. It was all I could do to drag around the dining room and check on the three customers that remained in my area. There was an older black man with a salt-and-pepper beard and rumpled clothes who'd been nursing the same cup of coffee for two hours, there was a college-aged black couple who were just finishing up a shared breakfast platter, and then there was a middle-aged white woman who was sipping warm tea and eating a toasted bagel with cream cheese. Once I knew everyone was okay, I headed to the kitchen to get a quick drink of water. Before I could make it to the kitchen, I heard dishes crashing behind me. I turned and saw that Ronnie had dropped a tray of food. I rushed over to him, crouched down, and began helping him clean up. From behind me I could hear Aunt Iris shrieking about the money she was losing because of the mishap.

In the middle of all of the chaos, no one noticed the man when he walked in the front door. No one noticed the gun in his hand, either. It wasn't until the female member of the college-aged couple screamed that we noticed him at all. My eyes widened as he raised the gun.

"What do you want? Money? I'll get you the money!" Aunt Iris screamed. As she turned toward the cash register, he shot her in the back. I watched her fall to the floor and then looked up at the man who still held the gun. As if in slow motion, I watched as Ronnie fell to the floor and held his mother. I stood to my feet. The patrons screamed and ducked underneath tables, but I just stood there—frozen.

I looked at the man as he turned around and aimed the gun at the middle-aged white woman. Finally, my mind registered what was going on, and I turned to run into the kitchen. I'd almost made it to the door when I heard the man say, "Where you think you going?!" In a split second I heard another gunshot and felt a searing pain in the side of my head. Then everything went black.

CHAPTER FIVE

"What a Difference a Day Made"

I woke up with the worst pain in the side of my head. I rolled over on my side and clutched my head. Was I bleeding? I looked at my hand. No blood, but my hair felt funny. It felt silky straight, like it'd been permed or straightened. I slowly sat up in the bed and looked at myself in the frosty mirror. Same mahogany skin, deep-set, dark brown eyes, angular cheekbones, and full lips, but my hair was in soft waves all over my head. What the hell? Where was my 'fro? Who did my hair while I was asleep? And what in the world was I wearing? I looked down at the floral-patterned dress and rubbed my hand across the shiny metal buttons that held it together at the front. It looked like one of my Grandma Loma's old housecoats.

I glanced around the dimly-lit room, *my* room, at the furniture. The room had once been my grandmother's and it still held the antique dresser, high boy, and bed that were once hers. There was a gardenia in a mason jar sitting on the dresser. *Who put that there?* I wondered. I squinted as the throbbing in my head became more apparent. I glanced down at the chenille bedspread and then further down at the brown shoes that sat on the floor next to the bed. *Whose shoes are those?* They were unattractive to say the least. They could've passed for Mary Janes, but not quite. They were more like Buster Browns with heels.

The room was so dim. I felt of my head again and this time brushed my fingers across a thick bandage. Then I remembered. I'd been shot, hadn't I? Had I been to the hospital and back without even realizing it? And why was I wearing this old duster? As I pondered my situation, my cousin Linda walked in wearing a hideous floral print dress with puffy capped sleeves.

"You all right?" she asked.

"I don't know. Why're you dressed like that? Is that one of Aunt Iris's dresses?"

Linda placed her hand on my forehead. "What you talkin' about? You feverish? You ain't makin' no sense."

I frowned. Linda was an English major and spoke perfect English. "Why are you talking like that, Linda?"

"That's it. I'ma tell Miss Loma to call a doctor. You talkin' outta yo' head." She turned to leave.

"Wait, what do you mean, Loma? My grandmother is dead."

Linda stopped dead in her tracks. "That may be so, but Miss Loma ain't your grandmother, I ain't got no Aunt Iris, and my name ain't Linda. That bump on your head musta knocked all the sense out of it. You need a doctor."

I was so confused that the throbbing in my head began to intensify. "What are you talking about? You're Linda, my cousin. This is our grandmother's house and your mother, Iris Townsend, is my aunt."

She stared at me for a minute, then left the room and closed the door behind her. I could hear her as she shouted, "Miss Loma, Junie done lost her mind!"

Junie? Who the hell is Junie? I stumbled to my feet and instantly fell back onto the bed. I was more than a little off balance. I sat on the side of the bed and stared at the floor. What happened to the carpet? In its place was dull hardwood flooring. *What in creation is going on?!* My head snapped up when the door flung open and in walked an absolutely beautiful woman. She was about my height with a figure that would put Kim Kardashian to shame. She was so beautiful, with flawless light brown skin and long, thick, wavy black hair. Her lipstick was bright red. Her black-brown eyes were full of concern as she approached me.

She smoothed the skirt of her navy blue polka-dotted dress and sat down beside me on the bed. She felt of my forehead and said, "You ain't got no fever. You feeling all right, Junie?"

"Who are you?"

"I'm Loma, sugar. You don't remember me?"

I slowly shook my head and then turned my gaze towards Linda, who was standing in the doorway. Loma followed my gaze. "That's Lila. She stay across the hall. Don't you remember?"

"Lila?" I said. I was near tears. Nothing was making sense.

"Yes. That's Lila Blanchet. I'm Loma Charles."

I frowned. "Loma Charles was my grandmother's name."

It was Loma's turn to frown. "Well, you never told me that before. Maybe we some kin."

"This is my grandmother's house. My Aunt Iris owns it now. Where is she?"

Loma took my hand. "Junie, sugar, this is my house. It belonged to my daddy before me. Nathan Charles. He was a white man," she said proudly. "I don't know no Iris, but that sho' is a pretty name. Huh, Lila?"

Lila nodded slowly. "It's a nice name," she said softly. "You think she need a doctor?"

"I don't know. Maybe…" Loma said.

"Why do you keep calling me Junie?"

Loma tilted her head to the side. "Because that's your name. Junie Walker."

I shook my head, aggravating the pain. "No, my name is J'Nay Walker."

Lila rolled her eyes. "I guess you done got fancy now. That bump on your head got you thinking you French or something? Or at least Creole? You know you ain't from no Louisiana."

"Wasn't I shot?" I asked.

Loma shook her head. "Oh no, sugar. You got in the middle of a fight downstairs. Got right in the way when Harry was 'bout to hit Lou Webster in the head with a whiskey bottle. He got you but good. Hit you right on the side of your head. No surprise you kinda out of sorts. You hungry?"

I nodded. "Why is it so dark in here?"

"Lila, go downstairs and fix Junie up a plate. If she can eat, she don't need no doctor." Loma stood from the bed and walked across the room, her white t-strapped shoes thudding against the wooden floor. "Let me open these curtains. Put some more light in here."

When she opened the drapes, I almost fell off the bed. Outside the window didn't look like Little Rock. Hell, it didn't even look like the year 2015. What was going on? "Where am I?" I asked as I stumbled across the room to the window. "And how did I get here?"

She placed her hand on my shoulder. "This my house... and you live here, remember?"

I closed my eyes and then opened them as if the mere act would change the scene outside my window. "No, what town is this?"

Loma frowned. "New Orleans."

"What? How did I get here?"

"Maybe I *should* call the doctor..." Loma said. She said some other stuff, too, but by then I'd tuned her out. I stared at the scene on the street below. There were trolley cars and old vehicles ambling along. When I say old, I mean *old*. Old like as in Shirley Temple-movie old. The people, mostly black people, wore old-fashioned clothes. "It… it looks like Rampart Street," I whispered.

Loma nodded. "That's right! Rampart Street. You remember!"

Lila walked in with a plate full of something that was steaming hot and smelled delicious. "Here we go," she said, placing the plate on the dresser. Loma guided me back to the bed, placed a napkin and the plate in my lap, and said, "Eat up, shug." Shug had always been how my grandmother addressed me. For the first time, I took a good look at Loma. A real good look. And I saw it. I saw *her*. She was an exact replica of the woman I'd seen in the pictures my grandmother had shown me. Pictures of her as a young woman. Could this really be my grandmother? If so, how?

I looked down at the plate full of dirty rice and étouffée and said, "Did you cook this, Loma?"

She smiled. "Of course. Who else gon' cook around here?"

"What year is it?" I asked.

"Well, 1939 of course." She rubbed my arm. "You can have the night off. You need to eat and get some rest."

1939?

She smiled down at me and turned to leave.

"You got any peach cobbler?" I asked.

She laughed. "You gon' be just fine. I'll send you up a bowl."

I spooned up a heaping helping of étouffée and breathed in the heavenly aroma. At that point, I decided that I had definitely been shot and that I must've died and gone to Heaven. Only in Heaven could the food smell this good. Yeah, that was it. I was in Heaven with my grandmother. I hoped to see my mama soon. I took a bite and closed my eyes. Yep, I was definitely in Heaven.

Chapter Six

"New Orleans"

I woke up with a start. The room was pitch black and very still. Eerily quiet. So what had awakened me? I lay still, listening and wondering. Had I been transported from Heaven to Hell or something? That's when I heard the music. Horns were blaring and a piano's keys were trilling loudly—upbeat jazz, the likes of which I'd never heard before. I stumbled to my feet and slid them into the shoes that sat next to my bed. I opened the door and my room partially filled with the light from the hallway. Placing my hand on the bandage that still covered the side of my head, I slowly stepped out into the familiar hallway and cautiously made my way to the staircase. With every step, the music grew louder and louder. At the bottom of the stairs, I took in the scene with awe.

There were wall-to-wall black folks. The women were dressed to the nines in flouncy dresses and hats with feathers, long white gloves on their hands and big gaudy rings on their fingers. They wore bright red lipstick and rouge, and nursed glasses of brown liquor. The men wore suits and hats and looked like they'd just stepped out of a gangster movie. Loma was behind the bar smiling brightly and pouring drinks. Linda, or Lila, was dressed in a tight little gold dress and was walking around hawking cigarettes. She spotted me and headed my way. "What you doing out of bed?"

"The music woke me up," I said.

"Well, if you gon' be down here, you need to get dressed and help me. Shoot, it's too many people in here for just me and the other two girls. And these old men is dirty. Grabbin' and feelin'. Ugh!"

I couldn't help but smile. Men were men, whether it was 1939 or 2015. And apparently whether in Heaven or on Earth. Men were men. "I wouldn't know what to do," I said.

"Mm-hmm. You done forgot, huh? That bump on yo' head done gave you amnesia. You better get on back up them stairs." With that, she pasted on a smile and resumed her work.

I leaned against the banister and continued to take in the scene. The little band was playing their hearts out and they sounded real good, too. They all had their hair in waves and wore black slacks, white shirts, and white suspenders. If I wasn't sure I was dead, I would've wanted to sing with them. Instead, I was content to tap my foot to the music.

The place smelled of cigarettes, hard liquor, and sweat, just like any other club I'd ever been in. The only difference was the music. I'd never heard so much heart and soul in my life! Those guys made you feel like they were connected to the music. Like those trumpets and saxophones were extensions of their very beings. I closed my eyes and felt the emotional connection they were sending with every note. It was so beautiful and so wonderful that I wished it was real. I wished it really was 1939 and that I was alive and I could know these men. I wanted to know what was behind the music, what made them play so well.

But they were ghosts. We all were and what difference did it make if I knew their secret if I would never be able to use it? I opened my eyes when I felt the heat of another person beside me. It was my cousin, Ronnie, I guess. At that point, I couldn't be sure. "Ronnie?" I said cautiously.

"Junie, it's me, Harry. I'm sorry 'bout hitting you in the head. Now you don't even remember me." He shook his head. "I'm so sorry, Junie. Can you forgive me?"

I sighed. "Yeah, it's cool. It's not like you were trying to do it." Nice answer since I had no recollection of the event.

We stood there in silence for a minute, and then he said, "You wanna dance?"

Okay, I didn't care who he was in this alternate universe or wherever I was, but he was my first cousin, Ronnie, in my world and there was no way I was dancing with him. Especially since the song the band was playing was a slow one. So I said, "No, I'm still feeling kind of shaky. I better go back to my room."

His face fell. "Oh, okay. See you later then, Junie."

I nodded and watched him walk away. I guess my lie was

convincing even to me, because I really did begin to feel woozy. I took another look at the room, smiled, and headed back up the stairs.

♫

"Rise and shine, sleepy head." The voice was cheerful and light and it reminded me of my mother's voice. Maybe she'd found out I was in Heaven and had come to visit me. I opened my eyes and smiled. "Mama?" I said softly.

She laughed and it was my Mama's laugh, and when I saw her face, she looked like a slightly lighter-skinned, younger version of my mama, but she said, "Child, I ain't nobody's Mama, and I never will be. I don't even like kids. You know that, Junie." Right then I decided that she definitely was not my mother. She, of all people, would know how to correctly pronounce my name.

I sat up on the side of the bed and said, "Who are you?"

She stopped in the middle of opening the curtains and looked at me. "Yeah, Loma said you was a little out of it. I'm Jessie, Loma's sister."

Great Aunt Jessie.

I'd never met my grandmother's sister, my mother's aunt. Neither had my mother. Great Aunt Jessie had been a wild one and had died young at the hand of a lover's jealous wife, or at least that's what my grandmother had told me. She was beautiful, just like Loma. I guessed that the white man was her daddy, too, judging from her light skin. My mama had been named after her Aunt Jessie.

"Oh," I said.

"Well, let me get you some water so you can wash up and come on down for breakfast. Loma said since you felt well enough to make it down the stairs last night and flirt with Harry, you can come on down for breakfast."

I frowned. "Flirt? I wasn't flirting with him. He's my… he reminds me of one of my cousins."

Jessie laughed again. "Hell, that don't mean nothing. Half the folks I know is married to they kin folk."

I shrugged. "Well, I don't believe in it."

"Good old Junie. Always doing what's right, huh? Maybe if I was more like you, I could keep myself out of some of this trouble I keep seeing my way into." She paused and then said, "I'll be back with your water."

Jessie left and I walked over to the old chifferobe and inspected its contents. Why on Earth did my clothes have to be so hideous? I mean, if I was in Heaven, where was my white robe? These dresses were so dowdy. Junie must have been a true spinster.

I was deciding between the ugly polka-dotted dress and the ugly floral-print dress when Jessie returned to my room with the wash basin and matching pitcher. You know, the kind you find in the antique stores? I smiled slightly. I hadn't seen one of those in a while. The only one my grandmother had owned she'd left behind when she moved away and it was lost in the hurricane. "Thank you," I said.

"You welcome. Wash up, now. Loma's cooking up some good breakfast."

"I bet she is."

Thirty minutes later, I was finished washing up, and having settled on the polka-dotted dress, I dressed and headed down the stairs. From the kitchen the aroma of what promised to be a delicious breakfast flowed throughout the entire house. Young Loma was just as good a cook as Grandma Loma, if not better. I sat down at the table and eyed the people surrounding me. There was Loma, still at the stove, dressed in a black skirt and a frilly white blouse with a pink apron on. She was wearing black heels as she fried eggs with expertise. Lila was already seated at the table as was Jessie. There were a couple more girls at the table who, of course, I didn't recognize.

I placed a cloth napkin in my lap and rubbed my hand across the bandage on my head.

"Does it hurt?" one of the girls asked. She had skin the color of dark chocolate and she was beautiful with slanted dark eyes and full lips. Her hair fell in ringlets around her face. I stared at her for a moment and then said, "Not really."

Lila patted my shoulder. "That's Esther. You remember her, don't you? And that's Betty," she said, pointing to the other girl. Betty was short and thin, almost bird-like with huge eyes. She was about my color and she wore her fine hair slicked to her head. "They work and live here like us," Lila added.

I offered them an awkward smile and then turned my attention to Loma, who was setting the food on the table.

"That's all right. It'll all come back to you. That's a nasty bump you got on your head. No wonder you been forgetting some things. How you feeling? You think you can work tonight?" Loma asked.

I shrugged. "I guess so if you tell me what to do."

"Just sell the cigarettes and help out serving drinks like always. It ain't hard. It'll come back to you in no time. Besides, we really need you back out on that floor. 'Specially since Betty went and got herself in trouble. She gon' have to go to bed after a while."

Betty dropped her eyes in shame and at the same time, rested her hand on her protruding stomach.

Loma eyed her for a moment and then returned her attention to me. "So anyway, we expecting some fellas from out of town tonight. Supposed to be a real good band. They just travelling through, but they wanna stop in and play at Loma's place while they here. Probably wanna spend a few nights, too, so you girls gon' have to share a room."

Esther's eyes widened. "All four of us?"

Loma nodded. "Well, yeah. That'll free up three rooms, four with Jessie's. A lot of money to be made from these fellas and I ain't missing out on it. They got their choice of Negro establishments to stay in, but they chose mine 'cause it's the best."

Everyone at the table nodded.

"Well, y'all eat up. Don't let this food go to waste. Them eggs expensive as hell. Cost me almost 30 cents a dozen. I'ma have to start raising some hens or something."

I stifled a giggle. Aunt Iris would dance a jig if she could get a dozen eggs for 30 cents.

We all dug in and ate in silence because it would have been disrespectful to talk while eating food that good. There were fried eggs, of course, and ham steaks, biscuits with sausage gravy, and thick pancakes with maple syrup. I would be full for days off of that breakfast, but I knew I'd have to have some of the black-eyed peas Loma announced she was cooking for dinner.

After breakfast, I went up to Lila's room so that she could "refresh" my mind on the duties of working at Loma's club. She filled me in on all of my duties and all of the do's and don'ts.

"Cigarettes is ten cents for a whole pack. Now, they gon'

try to argue about the price, but that's the same price the white folks is charging. It's two pennies for a single cigarette. Drinks is ten cents for three fingers. We outta rye liquor so you gon' get some complaints. Just tell 'em Wren be through with some more next week and that they gon' have to settle for gin or bourbon."

I nodded as I tried to take in her instructions.

"Remember to smile and be nice. That way at least some of these cheap bastards will tip you. But don't be *too* nice. You'll have them fools thinkin' they can get something you ain't gon' let them have." She lowered her voice and added, "Then you'll be like Jessie and have some crazy woman chasing you down Canal Street over her man."

My eyes widened. "That really happened?"

"Yeah, and she almost caught her, but Jessie is fast as hell to be so big-boned."

I smiled and fought back a giggle. "Okay, anything else I need to know?"

She shook her head. "Naw, it'll all come to you once you get back out there."

Well, that was doubtful, but I just nodded and said, "Okay. Thank you."

"Now, let me take this bandage off and try to do something with your hair. Can't make no money with this thing on your head."

CHAPTER SEVEN

"Jive at Five"

I spent most of the day moving my stuff into Betty's room at the end of the hall and helping Lila and Esther move their stuff in there, too. We decided that Betty would sleep in the bed since she was pregnant and then we flipped a coin to decide who would share the bed with her. Lila won the coin toss which meant that Esther and I would make a pallet on the floor.

Around five that evening, the band Loma spoke of arrived just in time to have dinner with us. We moved some of the tables together in the club and made one big, long table for them and served them the black-eyed peas, fried okra, smothered steak, and cornbread Loma had fixed. It seemed that even in death, I was a waitress.

The band was from the east and they were all very handsome and very nice, but when I saw the trumpet player sitting at the table, I nearly dropped the two plates I was holding. "John?" I said to the man who looked exactly like John Folks, except he looked better. Somehow, he was a more handsome version of John Folks in his suit and tie with a beanie hat atop his head. He possessed the same round eyes, wide nose, and nice lips, but the glasses he wore made him seem intelligent and introspective and his neatly trimmed soul patch made him look hip.

"You know John?" one of the other band members asked. "John, you know this fine lady?"

John gave me a confused look and shook his head. "No, I don't know her. But I *want* to know her." He smiled a brilliant, dimple-accented smile. His eyes were smiling, too. "What's your name, lovely?"

I just stood there and stared at him. It was John's voice coming from his mouth, but it was laced with something I had never associated John Folks with—confidence. "J'Nay," I finally said after Lila nudged me.

"That's a beautiful name for a lovely woman," he replied.

"*We* call her Junie," Lila said with a smirk.

"And we call old John here Dizzy," John's bandmate said.

I frowned slightly. "Dizzy?" One thing was for sure, this alternate universe John was making me *feel* dizzy. Something about him was truly magnetic.

John stood from the table and extended his hand. Once I took it, he brought my hand to his lips and softly kissed it. "John 'Dizzy' Gillespie at your service."

Dizzy Gillespie! THE Dizzy Gillespie?! "Mr. Gillespie?" I said breathlessly.

He grinned and glanced around the room before settling his gaze on me again. My heart fluttered. "No, baby, just call me

Dizzy or John. Hell, you can call me anything but *Mr. Gillespie*."

The other men laughed. I dropped my eyes. He was still holding my hand in his, and the realization that a jazz legend was touching me overwhelmed me. "Uh… sorry," I said as I pulled my hand away. "Excuse me." I scurried back into the kitchen and tried to catch my breath.

Lila was right on my heels. "You okay, Junie-uh, J'Nay?"

I shook my head. "That's Dizzy Gillespie out there," I whispered.

"Yeah, that's his name. Cute, ain't he?"

"He's more than cute. He's… he's *Dizzy Gillespie*."

Lila raised her eyebrows. "You heard him play before or something?"

I nodded as my mind reverted to the volumes of jazz albums my grandmother once owned. "Yeah, you could say that."

"He any good?"

"He's the best… the best."

Betty came in with a grin on her face. "Esther done set her eyes on one of the band members, that John man," she announced.

Lila gave her a smirk. "Honey, she better pick another one. From what I can tell, that John man ain't got eyes for no one but Junie, and she *sho' nuff* got eyes for him, too."

I didn't protest. Wasn't any sense in lying. I definitely had eyes for *this* John.

♪

Since Dizzy and his band would be playing that night, I didn't mind squeezing my body into the tight, little gold dress and hanging that heavy wooden cigarette box around my neck. Shoot, I would've done most anything to get to hear *the* Dizzy Gillespie play his horn.

My smile was genuine as I walked through the crowded room selling cigarettes and taking drink orders. Since I had experience in the service industry, it was easy to catch on, but Lila was right about one thing, the men were some hound dogs! Patting and poking and gripping with no respect for the women seated at the tables with them. It took all of my might not to pop one of those men upside his head. The level of disrespect was ridiculous!

When the music began, I stopped in my tracks, my eyes glued to the men on the small stage playing music without the aid of powerful speakers or special acoustics. There were no bright lights or videos screens. This was 1939, and this was *real* music played by *real* musicians. I stood there in the middle of the floor with a drink in each hand and closed my eyes and just listened. And then Mr. Dizzy Gillespie began to play a rapid succession of notes that matched the beat of the drums. I kept my eyes closed and tapped my foot to the rhythm. For a moment, time stopped. For a brief second, I believed that what was happening was real. I was Junie Walker and I was standing in a room full of well-dressed black people, and the one and only Dizzy Gillespie was playing his horn. But I was experiencing something I had never and would never experience in real life. In 2015, Dizzy Gillespie was long since gone on. But here in Heaven, he was blessing my ears like they'd never been blessed before.

I felt a little nudge and opened my eyes to find Lila staring at me with irritation on her face. Then she glanced around the room at the clamoring patrons and raised an eyebrow. I gave her a sheepish look and went back to work, tapping my feet and swaying my hips to the music all the while.

CHAPTER EIGHT

"After Hours"

There were only two toilets in Loma's house, and with the addition of the five band members, they became a scarce commodity. I had to resort to getting up in the middle of the night to do my business just to be sure there wasn't a line waiting outside the door when I was done. Their first night there, I crept from my pallet on Betty's floor to the bathroom around 2:00 A.M. I had finished doing my business and was quietly tipping back to bed when a voice startled me.

"Why, if it isn't the lovely one."

I jerked my head around to see John—Dizzy walking out of my room, slowly moving towards me. In the dim hall lighting he seemed even more handsome. I fought to calm my racing heart.

"You're in my room," was all I could think to say.

He turned and looked at the room and then back at me with a smile on his face. "That's your room, lovely? It's a nice room, but I sure wish you were in there with me."

I dropped my eyes, rubbed my warm cheeks.

He slid past me on his way into the bathroom. "See you later, lovely."

I watched as the bathroom door closed behind him and then

I climbed back underneath the covers next to Esther. I held my hand over my face to keep from giggling like a doggone school girl. How could I be dead and feel this excited and giddy about this man? I mean, he made me feel... *alive*. More alive than I ever felt when I actually *was* alive. It just didn't make sense.

When I closed my eyes, I still saw him—that smile and the sparkle in his eyes. I saw that swagger he had in his step, recalled the electricity I felt flowing between us as he passed me in the hall and when he kissed and held my hand the evening before. And his talent! His talent was by far the sexiest thing about him. Talent like that only comes around once in a lifetime and it is never duplicated again. The way he played his horn made me want to sing like I'd never sung before. It was just magical. But then again, he *was* Dizzy Gillespie, after all.

The next morning, all of us girls helped serve breakfast to the band before settling down in the kitchen to eat. I had a mouthful of biscuits and gravy and was staring down at a big, thick piece of bacon with the rind still on it when I noticed that everyone at the table had grown quiet. When I finally looked up, I saw that everyone was staring at the kitchen doorway. I followed their gazes to find Dizzy standing there holding his plate and a mason jar full of orange juice. I had intentionally avoided looking at him when I served the band breakfast, so the sight of him standing there in a crisp white shirt and baggy brown pants nearly took my breath away. The fact that he was staring right at me didn't help.

I quickly finished chewing my food and wiped my mouth with my napkin then placed it back in my lap. As I looked back up at him, he smiled at me, the thick hairs of his mustache and soul patch moving slightly to frame his mouth. I returned his smile and then dropped my eyes. Lord, that man was good looking!!

"You need anything, Mr. Dizzy?" Loma asked.

He nodded toward her and then fixed his eyes on me again. "Well, if you don't mind, I would like to eat in here with you lovely ladies."

Loma smiled as she glanced over at me. "Naw, we don't mind at all! Pull up a seat."

I watched him grab a chair from the side of the table opposite mine. It was Jessie's chair but she was nowhere to be found. According to Lila, that was not unusual for her. She had more than likely spent the night with someone she had no business being with. My heart flipped about three times when he pulled the chair around the table and squeezed it in between me and Lila. Lila eyed me and scooted out of his way.

Dizzy settled in his chair and looked over at me. "Good morning, lovely."

I gave him a timid smile. "Good morning, Mr.—Dizzy."

He grinned widely. "You sure are looking beautiful this morning."

I fiddled with the napkin in my lap and said, "Thank you."

I sat there beside him, feeling the warmth of his body next to mine as he ate his food and I stared at mine. There was no way I was going to eat another bite in his presence. God forbid I got something on my face or in the corner of my mouth. That would just be too embarrassing!

After breakfast, I volunteered to clean up the kitchen. I just needed some time alone and away from everyone to gather my thoughts. I needed to figure out what about Dizzy made me feel so shy and vulnerable and like... a woman.

I was up to my elbows in dishwater and deep in thought when I felt a hand on my back. I jumped and turned to see the source of my confusion standing next to me.

He gave me a small smile. "Did I scare you, lovely?"

"Uh-yeah-yes, you-you startled me. I didn't hear you come in."

"The other guys are going to check out the city today. I thought I'd see if you needed some help."

My eyes were glued to his lips. "H-help? Help with what?"

He nodded his head toward the sink. "The dishes."

I glanced at the sink and back at his mouth. "No-no, I'm fine. I don't need any help."

He gave me one of his smiles and then leaned in closer to

me. "Come on, let me help you, lovely." His voice was soft and smooth and unsettling.

I stopped breathing for a full minute and when I started back, I drew in a deep breath and slowly let it out before saying, "Okay."

He rolled up his sleeves and submerged his hands in the sink next to mine, ever slightly touching the fingers of my left hand. I quickly recoiled and turned to dry my hands on a dish rag lying on the kitchen counter.

"I like you, J'Nay," he said as he began washing a plate. I turned and looked at him. His eyes were glued to me. "I like you a lot," he added.

I opened my mouth and then closed it. *You're already dead. What difference does it make if you tell him how you feel?* "I like you, too. Dizzy," I admitted.

He pulled his hands from the sink, walked over to me, and gently kissed my cheek. And then he resumed washing the dishes. I stood there and watched him with a smile on my face.

♫

When I finally went upstairs after breakfast, everyone, and I do mean everyone—Loma, Betty, Esther, and Lila—was waiting for me in Betty's room. As soon as I walked into the room, Loma closed the door behind me and placed her hand on my arm. "Be careful with that Dizzy, Junie."

I frowned slightly. "Huh—why?"

She led me to the bed and sat me down beside Betty who looked like she was already tired enough to go back to bed. "He's a musician, shug. He's just passing through. Ain't nothing ahead for you but heartache if you start up with him."

I shrugged. "Who said I was starting up with him?"

"The look on your face every time you see him says it," Lila said. "But I can't lie, that is one fine, fine man!"

"Yes, he is!" Esther agreed.

Loma waved her hand. "Plenty of fine men 'round here to choose from. Don't make sense to fall for a musician. No good is gon' come of that. Take it from me. I know."

I stared at Loma for a minute and tried to remember what she and my mother had told me about my grandfather— Loma's husband. He was long gone by the time I was born so I'd never known him. And I don't think I ever really knew what happened to him. The only thing I did remember about him was his name—Otis Bezet.

"I guess you can talk since you got a good one. Shoot, Loma, you got Wren wrapped around your little finger," Lila said.

Loma rolled her eyes. "If he wrapped around my finger, why am I paying the same price for my liquor as everyone else. Naw, Wren ain't the one. He jus' good to keep company with from time to time. My real man is out there, I jus' hope he ain't already taken. I don't have no time for that mess Jessie be doing."

Everyone agreed. No one wanted be as reckless as Jessie. If only they knew what end Jessie was going to meet because of her actions. I shook my head slightly.

As if on cue, the door to Betty's room opened and in walked Jessie wearing one shoe, smeared lipstick, and a black eye.

Loma sprung to her feet. "Jessie! What happened to you?!"

Jessie stumbled over to the bed and perched at the head then reached down and pulled her shoe off. "Dexter Toussard happened to me. That Negro got mad about something I said and the next thing I know, I got a black eye and no ride home. I tell you right now, that's the last time he has the pleasure of my company."

Loma sighed. "I hope you mean it this time, Jessie. He ain't a bit of good. And he got a crazy wife—a crazy *white* wife!"

"Hmm, she'd have to be crazy to marry a black man," Esther mumbled.

"Oh, hell, that white woman ain't gonna do nothing to nobody. I ain't worried about her," Jessie said.

Loma wagged her finger at Jessie. "Well, you *should* be worried. She white and white folks think they rule the world. She ain't gonna be too happy to find out her man is messing around with a colored woman."

Jessie stood to her feet, and after she caught her balance, placed her hands on her thick hips and smirked. "I ain't colored, I'm *mulatto*."

"You got any Negro in you, you colored. You know that," Loma countered.

Jessie walked toward the door. "Humph. I'ma go wash up. Be glad when I can have my room back. Tired of sleeping in your room, Loma."

"Hell, it ain't like you sleep here, anyway," Loma said as she followed her out of the room.

Lila, Esther, and I all shook our heads as we watched them leave.

CHAPTER NINE
"Round Midnight"

One thing I already knew about the service industry was that in order to have a good shift, you had to be prepared. So later that afternoon, I went down to the first floor to survey the club in the daylight and get a better feel for the layout. In my mind, I was working out the best routes from the bar to each table and trying to find a spot where I could both hide from the patrons and rest my feet from time to time. Hopefully, things would feel less hectic this way. I softly hummed a tune as my eyes swept over the room.

"That's a lovely voice you got there, girl. I might have to start calling you 'songbird.'"

I jumped a little, startled by Dizzy's voice. "You could hear me? I didn't think I was that loud."

"You weren't loud at all, lovely. I just got good ears when it comes to music. I heard you all the way from upstairs. Left a good card game to see where that heavenly sound was coming from."

I tilted my head to the side. "You couldn't hear me from up there."

He rubbed his hand over his wavy hair and then rubbed his chin as he approached me. "You might be right. Maybe I just wanted to see you."

My heart felt like it was jumping rope in my chest. *How in the world do I still have a heartbeat if I'm dead?* "Oh."

"Oh? You ain't much for words, huh? But you sure are pretty as a picture."

I smiled.

"Would it be too forward of me to ask if you already have a beau, lovely songbird?"

I looked up at him, willed myself not to stare at his lips. "No—I mean, no, I don't."

His eyes widened in surprise. "The men around here must be dumb as rocks. Letting a fine-looking woman like you walk around here alone like this? I might just have to do something to fix that."

I placed my hand on my chest. "Something like what?"

"Something like making you my woman."

I shook my head. "Can't do that. You're just passing through."

He nodded slightly as he reached up and touched my cheek. "Well, if you're my girl," he whispered, "I guess you'll have to come with me… or I'll have to stay."

Then he leaned in and softly kissed me on the lips. Every nerve, muscle, and blood vessel in my body vibrated, and my knees buckled ever so slightly. "Dizzy…" I said softly.

He backed away from me with an intoxicated look in his

eyes. "Call me John. I like the way you say it."

"John?"

He smiled. "Yeah, I like that."

"Dizzy, you holding up the game, man!" a voice shouted from upstairs.

He leaned in close to me again and smiled. "Damn, girl… you smell good."

"I'm not wearing any perfume."

"I didn't think you were."

"Oh… um… well, t-thank you."

He smiled at me again, then took my hand and squeezed it. "You welcome. Can I see you after the club shuts down tonight, lovely?"

I nodded. He could've asked me to jump into a school of sharks or rob a bank and I don't think I would've been able to refuse him.

I watched him swagger back up the stairs and then, for the first time in several minutes, I breathed.

♫

Dizzy… or John helped me and the crew clean up after the club closed that night. Or at least he trailed behind me pretending to help. When he would catch me empty-handed, he'd grab my hand and twirl me around. I'd giggle but after noticing Lila's death glare, I'd quickly get back to work. I was wiping a table when he decided to sit at it, cross his legs, and grin at me. I grinned back. Something about his playful nature just warmed my heart. It seemed that everything about him made me like him more and more by the second. Who knew that being dead could be so wonderful?

After everything was cleaned to Loma's specifications, everyone except for Dizzy and me went upstairs. It was late and my eyes were very heavy, but I wanted to be with him. I wanted that more than anything. As we sat at that table smiling at each other, I placed my hand on the table and he placed his hand on top of mine. He spoke of the rigors of traveling with the band, the prejudice they'd encountered, and the generosity of some folks who just loved good music. But more than anything, he spoke of his love for music and his love for playing music. He said he was born to play his horn, that it was all he ever wanted to do.

"What about you, lovely? What do you wanna do?" he asked.

"I wanna sing," I said without hesitation. Even in the afterlife, my greatest desire hadn't been quenched.

He turned my hand over and traced the inside of my palm with his fingertip. "Will you sing something for me now?"

Shyness hit me like a ton of bricks as I suddenly remembered who this man was. "Right here... now?" I asked.

"Yeah, baby. I wanna hear you sing for me." His eyes were glued to me, giving me his full legendary attention.

I took a deep breath, told myself that this was a chance I'd never had in life so I might as well go for it. I began to sing "Summertime" from *Porgy and Bess* just as I had with John Folks. One of my hands was encased in his and the other was in the air making small, imaginary loops and circles. I often did that when I sang. It was a nervous habit of mine. I closed my eyes after the first note because the way he was looking at me—like I was Lady Day, herself—was very nerve-racking. Midway through the song, I opened them to see that Lila, Betty, Esther, Loma, and the drummer from the band were all standing on the staircase staring at me. After I sang the last note, they applauded. Dizzy even stood from his chair and clapped. I smiled and thanked them.

Dizzy reclaimed his seat and grasped my hand again. "That was beautiful, lovely. *Beautiful*."

Before I could reply, someone began to beat on the front door and Lila said, "Who in the world is that?"

"Probably some drunk. Let me see," Loma said as she headed toward the door. She opened it and before she could say a word, a pale white woman with shiny chestnut hair and red lips flounced inside. She wore an expensive-looking dress and I knew she had to be hot in that mink stole. It was July.

"Where is he?" she asked in a thick accent. She sounded British.

"Where is who and who are you?" Loma asked. Evidently, her being white meant nothing to Loma—even in 1939.

"I am Katrina Toussard. My husband, Dexter, comes here frequently and I believe his black *whore* lives here—Jessie."

My ears stood at attention. Great Aunt Jessie? Katrina? Hurricane Katrina killed my mother. Was this some type of afterlife joke? Was this the woman who killed my great aunt? I honestly didn't hear another word that was said after that. I was shaken to my core, reminded of a tragedy that had forever altered my life. Was history doomed to repeat itself in death? Is that what death was? A constant reminder of the bad times. I looked at Dizzy. Or maybe it was a reminder of what I'd missed out on in life—love. Loma had words with Katrina and ushered her to the door and soon everyone, including me and Dizzy, went upstairs.

We stopped outside of Betty's door and he said, "Thank you for singing for me."

I looked into his eyes. "You're welcome."

He placed his hands on either side of my face and planted a long, lingering kiss on my lips. I reached up and gripped both of his arms and then wrapped my arms around him as I returned the kiss with fervor. His lips were like a balm to my soul and when he pulled me into an embrace and continued to kiss me, I wished I was alive so that I could give this man babies. It felt that good to be in his arms.

He finally released me and then kissed his own fingertip and placed it against my lips. "Goodnight, lovely songbird. Dream of me when you go to sleep."

"I will."

It wasn't a lie. John "Dizzy" Gillespie and his kisses dominated every second of my dreams that night.

Chapter Ten

"Jump, Jive an' Wail"

The next morning, Dizzy abandoned his bandmates again and joined us for breakfast. He sat so close to me that his thigh pressed against mine. Being that close to him made it hard for me to concentrate on eating my breakfast. The way he smelled, the sensation of his thigh touching mine, the warmth of his presence—all of that nearly sent me over the edge. If I didn't know any better, if I hadn't only met him a few days earlier, and if I wasn't dead, I'd think I was falling in love.

"This sure is some good food, Miss Loma. I think these are the best biscuits I've ever had!"

Loma smiled. "Why, thank you, Mr. Dizzy."

"Loma's the best cook in town, everybody knows that," Esther chimed in, fluttering her eyelashes at Dizzy. She sat on the other side of him and I'd noticed her eyeing him several times. *I don't know what her problem is, stepping in on my territory. She'd better watch herself.* As soon as those thoughts jumped into my head, I chased them away. What in the world was wrong with me?

I didn't have dish duty, so I walked out onto the front stoop for some fresh air. I'd only been standing out there watching the hustle and bustle of colored folks on Rampart Street for a few minutes when I heard the door open and close behind me. "Mind if I join you, lovely?"

I turned around and smiled despite myself. "I don't mind."

I lowered myself onto the top step, making sure to tuck my long dress around my legs. Dizzy sat down beside me, leaned in close, and planted a kiss on my cheek. "Sure is a beautiful day, isn't it?"

I nodded. It was a gorgeous day, but I assumed that every day was a gorgeous day in Heaven.

"What's on your mind, songbird?" he asked.

I turned and looked into his smiling eyes. "You wouldn't believe me if I told you."

"Try me."

I sighed and fixed my eyes on the street again as I shook my head.

"Okay, okay. I won't force you. I'll just sit out here and enjoy this weather and your beauty."

I glanced over at him and he flashed me a smile. "Are you always happy, John?"

"Don't see no point in being unhappy. Do you?"

Before I could answer, a voice broke into our little conversation. "Well, well. You out here courting the entertainment, Junie?" It was Jessie.

I sprung to my feet. "Jessie! Where you been?" She hadn't been home since before Katrina came looking for her.

Jessie looked surprised. "Out… with Dexter."

"I thought you were done with him!"

She frowned. "Well, that really ain't none of your business, now is it, Junie? Hell, you acting like Loma."

I tried to calm myself, but I'd been worried about her. I still was. "His wife came looking for you last night."

She bugged her eyes. "His who did what?"

"His wife came looking for you. Loma talked to her."

Jessie slid past me and Dizzy, who was now on his feet, too, and headed into the house. I moved to follow her, but Dizzy grabbed my arm and stopped me. "Hey, you okay, lovely?"

I looked at him and before I could stop myself, dissolved into tears. He pulled me to him and held me tightly. I guess I was just overwhelmed with the emotions of not really understanding why I was there, in that place and time. Or maybe the confusion over whether or not I was dead had finally gotten the best of me. Or maybe, just maybe, the thought of losing my mother again, in any form, was too much for me to handle. Whatever it was, the tears seemed to relieve it a little and being in Dizzy's arms made it even better.

♫

After all of the advice Loma gave me about not getting involved with Dizzy, it turns out she and the drummer, a fellow they called Muskrat, had gotten pretty close. Lila had gotten cozy with the pianist. Esther had even latched onto the clarinet player. Well, Loma was so giddy about her new beau, she decided to close the club down for the night—something Betty said never had happened—and throw a little private party for the band and us workers.

She pulled out her best liquor, cooked a big Cajun meal, and the band took to the stage for an informal performance. It felt so good to be able to sit at a table and enjoy the music without worrying about getting someone's drink order right or some old geezer trying to rub up against my butt. The atmosphere was loose and carefree. Liquor was flowing, sweaty bodies were swaying, voices were yelling, "Woo!" and "Yeah!" as they dipped and tipped around the small dancefloor. The music was spectacular, and Dizzy had never played or looked better than he did that night.

The only hitch was the fact that Jessie had invited her man, the infamous Mr. Toussard, to our little shindig. One look at him and I definitely understood why she found it so hard to leave him alone. Mr. Toussard was tall with smooth, milk chocolaty skin. His wide-set eyes were a deep brown and his thin moustache was neatly trimmed. He was dressed like a million bucks in a white suit, white tie, and matching white fedora. He looked like money, *old money*, and he oozed charisma. He greeted and kissed the hand of every woman in the room, including me. He was hands down, the best-looking man in the room, maybe the best-looking man in all of New Orleans at the time. A fine looking man, as Loma would put it. But in 2015 terms, he was just plain *fine*. But as fine as he was, his presence made all of us feel a little ill at ease. If my Dizzy hadn't been up on that stage making my heart flutter, I might have worried the night away.

But there he was, one of the greatest trumpeters in the history of music, his jaws inflated, his round eyes stretched wide, his fingers rapidly moving as he played along with his band. I clapped and bounced in my seat, wearing a smile so bright that it could have lit up all of Rampart Street in the dead of night. In the middle of one number, he left the small stage and played his way to where I sat. He stood at my table, one foot in a chair, and played while staring down at me. I stared right back, reveling in this private public performance. At that point, my heart beat for that man—it really did.

When the band finished blessing us, Loma cranked up her phonograph and old standards began to fill the room. I smiled as Dizzy made his way back to my table, wiping sweat from his brow with a handkerchief as he slid through the room, which was crowded with tables just like any other night. He stopped next to my table and reached for my hand. "May I have this dance, songbird?"

I smiled, took his hand, and let him lead me out to the dancefloor where Loma and Muskrat where already cheek to cheek. As Ethel Waters sang "Stormy Weather," Dizzy pulled me into his arms and we began to sway to the music. I closed my eyes, rested my head on his shoulder, and hummed along with Ethel. *If I really am dead, God, thank you for making Heaven such a wonderful place.*

When I opened my eyes, Dizzy was staring down at me with a grin on his face. "You got some kind of voice, songbird. Never heard a woman hum as pretty as you do."

I reached up and kissed his cheek. "Thank you, Diz— John."

His grin faded and his feet stopped, and right there on the dancefloor, in front of the band and everyone else, he leaned in and kissed me like I had never been kissed before—in life or death. It was a deep kiss full of desire and passion and longing. As I accepted his affection, I felt my heart begin to swell and my head begin to swim. At that moment, at that very second, I knew that—living or dead—I had fallen in love with John Gillespie. I also knew that I didn't ever want to know what it felt like to be without him.

"What the hell is going on in here?!" a voice boomed.

The voice snatched me from my utopian bliss and I turned to see that it belonged to my cousin, Ronnie, or Harry, or whoever he was.

He stomped all the way over to where Dizzy and I stood. "Get yo' hands offa her!"

I frowned. "What?"

Dizzy backed away, confusion and I think, a little hurt, on his face.

"Harry, you ain't got no right to come busting up in here like that!" Loma shouted. "That temper of yours is what got Junie hurt the last time."

"What I'm s'pose to do if I see another man kissing my woman, Loma?!"

I held up my hands. "Whoa, wait a minute. Who said I was your woman?"

Ronnie-Harry slapped his hand on his chest. "*I* said it. All the times I came up in here and bought this cheap liquor just so I could get to see you. Shoot, that fight with Lou Webster was over you! You s'pose to be mine, Junie! Mine!"

"What you mean, cheap liquor?! I serve nothing but high quality—"

Muskrat rubbed Loma's shoulder and whispered something in her ear to calm her and cut off her rant.

I shook my head. "I'm not your woman. I could never be your woman, Ron-Harry." *Because you are my cousin, or at least you look just like him.*

Dizzy stepped up. "Look, she said she not your woman—"

"You ain't nothin' but a two-bit hustlin' musician! You ain't gon' do nothin' but take her heart and break it. You gon' leave her behind and never come back. You need to leave her alone!"

Dizzy tilted his head to one side and with a slight grin said, "Now look here, cat. You don't know me—"

That's when Ronnie-Harry punched him—dead in the nose. I shrieked.

Dizzy punched him back, knocking him to the floor. Some of his bandmates stood to the side, egging him on. Loma grabbed me and pulled me away from the mêlée, but I kept my eyes glued to Dizzy who was putting the whooping of a lifetime on his opponent. The distinguished Mr. Toussard never moved a muscle. He just sat there with a cigar dangling from his lips and Jessie perched on his lap.

When the fight was over, Dizzy came to me with bloodied knuckles and wrapped his arm around my shoulders. "Let's take a walk, songbird."

I nodded and followed him outside while Harry lay a bloody mess on the dancefloor.

CHAPTER ELEVEN

"Fools Rush In"

Dizzy and I walked down the street hand in hand, taking in the sights that surrounded us—black folks dressed to the nines, filing in and out of jazz clubs and restaurants. I was in awe of their flawless appearances, their sense of pride. I wondered what had happened to make that fade away as the years passed. A well-dressed man was a rare commodity in 2015. A modestly dressed, elegant woman was even rarer.

I glanced over at Dizzy, who for the first time since I'd known him, was quiet, his face missing the smile that first reeled me in. "I don't know why Harry acted like that. I'm not his woman, Dizzy."

He stopped walking and turned to face me. "I know that. A woman like you wouldn't fool around with a hot head like him."

I was relieved to know that he believed me but I was still a little worried about his aloofness at the moment. "Then why are you so quiet tonight?"

He took a deep breath and released it. "Because… because most of what he said about me is true. At least it used to be."

"What used to be true?"

He brought my hand to his lips and kissed it for a long,

lingering moment. "I done broke a lot of hearts out on the road, lovely. A bunch of 'em. But things done changed now."

"Things changed how?"

"I found you and I think I'm falling for you, lovely. I can't get you outta my head or outta my heart."

I dropped my eyes and he placed his hand on my chin and lifted my face until my eyes met his. "How do you feel, lovely? How do you feel about me?"

"I... I like you, Dizzy. I like you a lot. I'll really hate to see you go when you do."

He dropped his hand and turned his back to me.

I reached for him then drew my hand back. "What's wrong?"

He faced me again. "I just expected more than that."

I frowned. "More than what?"

"Like? Hell, I *like* whiskey. I *love* you. I thought you loved me, too."

I backed away from him. "I... I do, but that doesn't make sense because..."

"Because what?"

"We..." *We're dead.*

He moved closer to me, rested his hands on my arms. "We what, baby?"

"I don't... I don't wanna..."

"You don't wanna love me?"

"No, I mean, yes. I mean, I already love you, Dizzy."

He grinned, pulled me to him, and gently kissed me. "That's all I need to know. I love you, too, lovely. I love you, too."

When I finally joined Esther on the pallet, my mind was in a fog. I lay there in the darkness and quiet, trying to figure out what was going on. Why would I die, be sent to a Heaven that resembled 1939, and be surrounded by people who looked like people from my life—including my own grandmother and great aunt? Or was this just a pit stop on the way to Heaven? Was there something I was supposed to be doing here? Did I have an assignment?

And why and how did I manage to fall in love with the one and only Dizzy Gillespie and if I was already in Heaven, was there a future here for us? Could we get married and have children in Heaven? Because that was all he made me want to do, and getting married and having children had been the furthest thing from my mind when I was alive. Shoot, I didn't even have any boyfriend prospects when I was alive, let alone husband prospects.

Well, that wasn't entirely true. There was John Folks, after all. But was he really a prospect? Sure, he looked like Dizzy, but he was so quiet and shy. But his smile, his smile was nice—not as dazzling as Dizzy's, but *nice*. I wondered if maybe, underneath his shyness, he was just as fun and appealing as Dizzy. *Maybe I should've given him a chance.*

I shook my head. It was too late for that. I was dead and I needed to figure out exactly what that meant for me... and for me and Dizzy.

♪

The next morning, as Dizzy sat next to me at the breakfast table, I couldn't stop myself from grinning. Between bites of food, he would wink at me or make some funny face that would send me to giggling like a teenager. Then I would glance around the table, notice that everyone was staring at me, and stop. But as soon as I did, he'd do something else to put a smile on my face. At one point, he scooted closer to me, pressing his thigh against mine as he stole a piece of bacon from my plate. Now, I loved me some Dizzy Gillespie, but I think I might've loved that bacon more. "Hey! That's mine," I protested.

"I know," he said and then he took a bite and placed the rest in my open mouth. I was in the middle of chewing and grinning when he kissed me.

"Lord, you two need to get a room!" Esther said as she rolled her eyes and threw her napkin onto her plate of half-eaten food. "Y'all act like y'all the only ones at this table."

1939 Hater.

Dizzy rolled his eyes and leaned in and kissed me again. I giggled again.

Esther huffed and stood from her chair. As she left, she ran right into Harry as he walked in and stared at me and Dizzy. It felt like all of the air left the room. *Please, not another fight.*

Loma stood from her chair. "Harry, I don't want no trouble in here today. This is my place of business and—"

Harry pulled off his hat and held up his hand. "No, ma'am, Miss Loma. I ain't here to cause no trouble. I owe you and everyone else here an apology. I'm real sorry for the way I acted last night. Real sorry."

Loma reclaimed her seat and nodded. "Well, thank you for your apology."

Harry turned to me, his face a bruised mess. "Junie, can I speak to you for a moment?"

Dizzy grabbed my hand and held it tightly in his. "Anything you got to say to her, you can say right here and now."

Harry dropped his eyes and stared at his hat. "Look, man. I know she yours now. I… I respect that. Just something I need to say to her in private."

Before either Dizzy or I could say a word, Jessie busted in the kitchen door with a big grin on her face. As soon as she saw the scene before her, she dropped the grin and said, "Oh, Lord. Y'all better put these dishes up, else we won't have a plate left to eat on."

Harry looked up at her and shook his head. "No, Miss Jessie. Ain't gon' be none of that. I'm here to apologize... and to talk to Junie."

Jessie raised her eyebrows. "Hell, I don't blame you for not wanting to fight. That Negro damn near beat the sense out of you!"

"Jessie!" Loma said.

"Junie, *please,*" Harry pleaded.

I sighed, looked over at Dizzy whose eyes were glued to me. I whispered to him, "It's okay."

Squeezing his hand, I stood from my chair. "All right, Harry, we can step outside."

I led Harry through the club, out onto the front stoop. Dizzy followed us all the way to the front door and when I tried to close it behind me and Harry, he blocked it and shook his head. He stood in the doorway as me and Harry moved down a step or two.

"I'm real sorry, Junie. I... just... it didn't set well with me when I saw you with that man in there. It didn't set well at all," he said softly.

I stared down at my feet. "Well, it's not really any of your business, Harry."

"I know. I just... all that time we flirted back and forth, I thought... I just thought..."

I sighed. Junie might have been working up to something

with him, but J'Nay sure wasn't. But there was no way I could get him to understand what was really going on with me without sounding insane. "I don't remember any of that, Harry. I'm sorry."

He looked at me, alarm registering on his face, quickly replaced by guilt. "You still can't remember?" He dropped his head and slowly shook it from side to side. "I'm so sorry. This is all my fault, then. It's my fault you wit' that cat."

I gently rested my hand on his arm. "No, Harry. I'm with him because I like him. It doesn't have anything to do with the bump on my head or my memory. I'm sorry things didn't work out between us."

Seeing my hand on Harry's arm, Dizzy stepped outside.

I dropped my hand and began to climb the steps. "Bye, Harry."

He looked up at me as Dizzy wrapped his arm around my shoulder and kissed my cheek. "Bye, Junie."

As soon as Dizzy closed the door behind us, a loud crash startled both of us. Everyone in the house came running to find a brick lying on the floor next to one of the tables. Someone had thrown it through the window.

Chapter Twelve

"Hot House"

Dizzy snatched the front door open, sure that Harry had been the culprit. He was halfway down the steps when Muskrat shouted, "There's a letter! It wasn't him, Diz!"

Dizzy rushed back into the house. We all surrounded Loma as Muskrat handed her the letter and she read it aloud. *"Stay away from my husband, black whore."*

Loma handed the letter to Jessie, who stared at it in her hands. "Dexter Toussard ain't welcome here no more," Loma said.

Jessie's head snapped up. "Why? 'Cause his wife is crazy? He ain't got nothing to do with this. And how you even know it's from his wife?"

Loma placed her hands on her wide hips and stuck her neck out. "'Cause he married and you don't have no business with him. And it's gotta be her because who else in here is sneaking around with somebody's husband? Now I gotta get my damn window fixed before we open up tonight. Let me call somebody." She made a step and then turned around. "Dexter got a phone at his house? You need to call him."

Jessie frowned. "For what?"

"He need to pay for my window." Loma left and Lila

rushed to the kitchen and came back with a couple of brooms. She and Esther cleaned up the glass while Betty sat at one of the tables rubbing her belly.

Dizzy grasped my hand and whispered in my ear, "Let's take a walk, lovely."

I hesitated, feeling a little guilty about leaving the other girls behind to deal with the clean-up. Then I decided that there really wasn't much I could do and they seemed to have everything handled. Plus, I felt a little out of sorts because of what had just happened. Katrina throwing that brick through the window was like an ominous sign of what was to come and I felt powerless to change it. I mean, what could I tell Jessie that would make her listen to me? That she was really my great aunt, and that her sister was my grandmother but my mother, who was her namesake, had not been born yet? That I was from the future and I knew for sure that Katrina was going to kill her? If I told her all of that, she'd think I was crazy. So would everyone else, including Dizzy.

Dizzy tugged on my hand, snatching me from my thoughts. I gave him a weak smile and followed him out of the front door. We walked hand in hand, passing by other couples or families. It was warm out but not too hot, and Dizzy's hand felt good in mine.

"A penny for your thoughts?" Dizzy said.

I glanced at him, saw the silly smile he was wearing, and I

couldn't stop myself from giggling.

He gave me a peck on the cheek. "Ah, I got you smiling again, huh? What's on your mind, lovely?"

I shrugged. "Nothing, really."

"Yeah, there is. You thinkin' 'bout what happened back at Loma's."

I dropped my eyes and nodded. "I'm kinda worried about Jessie. She doesn't seem to be worried but she should be."

He frowned and tilted his head to the side. "You really worried about her, ain't you?"

I nodded again. "I am. I think that woman, Katrina, is dangerous."

Dizzy stopped walking and looked at me. "She might be, lovely. But it ain't gon' do no good worrying about something you can't change. Jessie, that man, and his wife are all grown. They gon' have to deal with the choices they're making."

I stared at him for a moment, in awe. What he'd said was much more profound than I'm sure he even realized. And it was just what I needed to hear. "Thank you," I said as I pressed a kiss against his cheek.

He pulled me into his arms and kissed me deeply. When he released me, he said, "Now that's how you thank a man."

♪

"Junie... Junie!"

I thought I was dreaming the urgent, whispered voice until I felt someone shake me. My eyes popped open, took a moment to focus, and then settled on Jessie's face. Her brow was furrowed, and there was anxiety in her voice.

Esther stirred beside me. "What's goin' on?" she slurred, her eyes still clamped shut as she turned her back to us and resumed her slumber without waiting for an answer. It had been a rough night at the club, with the room full of demanding patrons and the uneasiness we all felt about the events from earlier that day looming over all of us. I knew she had to be tired. I was tired, too. But nevertheless, I left the semi-comfort of my pallet and followed Jessie from the room, down the hall, and down the stairs where she slumped into a chair and sighed.

I sat across from her. "What's wrong, Jessie?" I asked through a yawn. "You worried about Dexter's wife?" *I sure am.*

She nodded and then dropped her eyes. "I just need to talk to somebody. Can't talk to Loma. All she do is fuss. Lila too mean. Betty too dumb, and I just don't like Esther."

I stifled a smile. I seemed to remember Grandma Loma saying that Great Aunt Jessie was a little outspoken and straightforward. I saw the truth in that statement at that moment.

"My daddy dead. My mama, too. You the only one I can talk to, Junie," she said.

"Okay, then talk."

"I done messed up. I'm... I'm in the family way. And it's Dexter's."

"What?" I said as I leaned forward.

"I said, I'm gon' have a baby if that crazy white woman don't kill me first."

"Jessie, I..."

"I know. I know. It was dumb as hell for me to let myself get knocked up by a married man with a crazy wife. I don't know what I'm gon' do."

"Does he know?"

"Naw. I just really got sure about it myself today. And after what his wife did this morning, I'm kinda scared to tell him."

I gave her a sympathetic look. "You gotta tell him, Jessie."

She sighed again and then laid her head on the table. "I know, but I wish I could just go away from here. I know we got some family up north, our Mama's folks. But after Mama started courting our daddy and having babies by him, they wouldn't have nothing to do with her anymore. I don't even remember their names."

I sat there and stared at Jessie. She was a beautiful woman with thick, wavy hair and smooth, butterscotch skin. She was tall and statuesque. And despite the big talk she did day in and day out, at that moment, I knew she was scared. I wished I could help her, but I just didn't see how I could. Then I remembered something I'd heard my grandmother, my aunt, and my mother all say. *"Some things only God can fix, so you have to take them to him."*

She looked up at me. "What?"

I didn't realize I'd spoken the words aloud. "We need to pray for God to fix this," I said.

She gave me a skeptical look. "I ain't never been too much of a praying person, Junie. I didn't think you was neither."

I reached across the table for her hand. "My mama was always praying. I forgot about that. I..." *I forgot about a lot of things.* I'd been too busy trying to be a star.

"You what?" She asked as she took my hands.

"I need to pray more. Close your eyes, Jessie."

She closed her eyes and lowered her head. I prayed for Jessie's safety and her baby's safety. I prayed for her protection from Katrina. I prayed for Dexter to do right by her and her baby. Silently, at the same time, I prayed that I would never stop feeling what I felt for Dizzy. As we both left for bed, I wondered how prayer worked in Heaven. Was it the same as on Earth? Could God hear me?

As I settled under the covers next to Esther, I reasoned that prayers were probably more powerful in Heaven. After all, I was much closer to Him there.

♪

Kissing felt so good in Heaven! Okay, maybe that's a bad thing to say, but it's the truth. Or maybe it was just Dizzy's kisses that felt good, because Lord knows that man knew how to lay a kiss on you that would make you want to take off running and shouting. He made me want to shout like old Sister Lucette used to do in church when I was a little girl. Sister Lucette would buck and jump and scream so hard you would've thought the devil had her instead of the Holy Spirit. One time, she bucked so hard that she knocked one of those old pews right over. The whole pew! No one ever sat next to her because they knew better, so the pew was empty when it toppled over with a loud thud and fell on the feet of the people sitting behind her. Sister Lucette would shout for the better part of the sermon, and that's what I felt like doing right there on the staircase.

There I was in my tight little gold cigarette girl dress, heading down to work when Dizzy, trumpet in hand, stopped me and laid a kiss on me that everyone in the building should've been able to feel. I felt it in my lips and chest and, well... I didn't want him to stop kissing me, and I don't think he wanted to stop, either. But in the middle of our lip-lock, I felt him move away. I opened my eyes to see Muskrat pulling on him.

"Hey, man, it's show time," Muskrat said and then winked at me. "That pretty girl and her lips ain't goin' nowhere."

As Dizzy dashed down the stairs, he grinned at me. "We gon' finish that later, lovely."

I nodded and grinned and bopped down the stairs. But a good old Pentecostal shout was welled up in my soul. Dead or alive, I loved John "Dizzy" Gillespie.

Chapter Thirteen

"S' Wonderful"

Dizzy's arms were wrapped tightly around me as we sat on the bottom step in front of the house, our mouths connected, our hearts beating in unison. It was late, the club was closed, and though I could still hear the trill of piano keys and the be-bopping notes of Dizzy's trumpet ringing in my ears, the only thoughts in my mind were of how this man, *this John,* was making me feel right then and there. But those thoughts were followed by thoughts of the 2015 John—John Folks. Could things have been this good with him? Or could anything on Earth be as good as being with Dizzy in Heaven? As Dizzy finally backed away from me a little, he frowned slightly. "What's wrong?"

I shook my head and felt a tear trickle down my cheek. I hadn't realized I was crying. "Nothing." I said.

"Then why you crying, songbird?"

I shrugged slightly. "I don't know. This just feels so good. You and me—us together. I wish I knew what this felt like a long time ago. I wish I knew you before now."

He gently caressed my cheek. "You know me now, and we got forever to feel what we feel. I ain't letting you go. I... I want you to come with me when I leave."

"With you and the band? What will I do, I mean, when you're performing? And where will I sleep? Don't y'all share rooms and stuff?"

"You can sing with us! With your voice? Girl, we'll be a big hit! And you gon' sleep in the room with me, in the bed with me. As my wife. We gon' have our own room."

My mouth dropped open. "Your *wife*?"

"Yes, baby. *My wife.* I wanna marry you before we leave New Orleans. That way you'll have all your friends there to see."

"Wow, uh... I don't know what to say, Dizzy."

He gave me a slight grin. An irresistible dimple accented his cheek. "I was hoping you'd say yes."

I stared at him, my heart beating with more of a sense of purpose than it ever had before. I reached up and touched his dimple. Then I kissed his lips and said, "Yes."

A wide smile spread across his face. "Thank you. Things are gonna be good for us, lovely. I just know it! Nothing but sunshine and smiles in the future for us."

I giggled as he nuzzled my neck. He pecked me on the lips and then hopped to his feet, reaching for my hand. "Come with me, baby."

"Where we going?" I asked as he pulled me to my feet.

He didn't answer. He just led me to the sidewalk, took my hand, and twirled me around before pulling me into his arms and leading me in a dance with no music. I didn't resist. I just fell into step with him, leaning into him and closing my eyes. We danced for a long time to the rhythm playing in Dizzy's head. When I opened my eyes, I looked up and noticed the brightness of the full moon and the sky that seemed to be crowded with stars. I smiled. "I love you, John," I whispered.

He stopped dancing and cradled my face in his hands. "I love you, too, J'Nay."

♬

Harry joined us for breakfast the next morning, but he didn't say a word to either me or Dizzy. Instead, he sat very close to Lila. Evidently, they were suddenly an item now. I should've been a little concerned since they were brother and sister in my old life, but I was relieved. I was truly glad he'd moved on. He was too much like my cousin to be carrying a torch for me.

Dizzy fed me off and on throughout the meal and when he wasn't feeding me, I was feeding him, and when we weren't feeding each other, we were kissing or giggling. We may as well have been the only two people at the table because we were in our own lovely little world. We were totally oblivious to everyone else.

"Let's go get the rings today," Dizzy said softly.

I nodded. "Okay."

"Rings? Did I hear somebody say rings?" Loma asked. How she could hear us clear across the table with all of the forks and glasses clanking around us, I have no idea.

Dizzy took my hand and squeezed it. "Yeah, me and my lovely songbird gon' get married before we leave New Orleans. You know a preacher that'll marry us?"

I think everyone at the table gasped. Harry, who must've forgotten that he was supposed to be seeing Lila, jumped up from the table with a stricken look on his face.

Loma's mouth hung open for a second. "Uh... Junie, can I talk to you?" She stood from the table.

I leaned over and kissed Dizzy. "I'll be right back."

I followed Loma up into her room where she closed the door behind us. Then she turned to face me where I sat on the side of her bed. "Have you gone plum out of your mind, Junie?! You just met this man, and you gon' marry him! He's a *musician*!"

I shrugged. "So is Muskrat, but you sure have been spending a lot of time with him."

"I ain't gonna marry Otis Bezet, though! That's for sure!"

I frowned and my heart jumped at the mention of the grandfather I'd never known. "Who is Otis Bezet?"

"That's Muskrat's real name. He some kin to the Bezets from over in Monroe. Ain't that somethin'?"

I smiled. "You in love with him, and you gon' marry him one day, Loma."

"Lord, that bump on your head done scrambled your brains."

"No, my brain is fine. You're in love and so am I. I'm marrying Dizzy, because I love him."

"You can't love someone you barely know, Junie. Neither can I. This is just crazy!"

"Says who?" I asked. "Where is that rule written?"

"It's written in the minds of folk with common sense, which is what Harry obviously knocked out of you!"

I shook my head. "I love him. I know that for a fact. And he loves me."

Loma sat down beside me. "You worse than Jessie, wherever her behind is. Woke up early this morning and she'd already snuck off somewhere. You and her gon' be the death of me."

I looked at her and smiled. "Don't worry about me. I know what I'm doing."

"He's gonna hurt you, Junie."

"He can't hurt me. We're in Heaven."

She sighed as she shook her head. "You talking like a crazy woman right now. *Must* be in love."

"I am. I really am."

She reached up and rested her hand on my cheek. "Then I

hope he always makes you as happy as you are right now."

She hugged me and I said, "Thank you. I know he will."

As we stood to leave the room, she grabbed a hat and put it on her head. "Will you clean up the kitchen for me? I gotta step out for a little bit."

I nodded. "Sure. Where you going?"

"Down to my mama's old church to see if Reverend Bozant will marry you and Mr. Dizzy."

I hugged her again. "Thank you! Thank you, Loma!!"

Chapter Fourteen
"My Heart Stood Still"

The Reverend Ezra Bozant was a short, wide man with light skin, beady little black eyes, and a long nose. His breathing was labored and he wheezed between just about every word he uttered. But you would've thought the illustrious Reverend Martin Luther King, Jr. or the Reverend Jessie Jackson was officiating my wedding judging from the grin that never left my face. Dizzy and I were married right in Loma's club at the foot of the stairs. Loma had let me borrow one of her expensive dresses. It was a beautiful white dress with a lacy scooped neck, puffy sleeves, A-line skirt, and a pale yellow ribbon that tied around the waist. She also lent me a pair of white sandal heels and a set of pearl earrings. Atop my head sat a white pill box hat. Dizzy stood next to me in a black suit, looking good enough to eat with a grin on his face accentuating those irresistible dimples of his.

We said our vows in the company of everyone I knew in Heaven, and I could feel the love and good vibes coming from each one of them. When we were pronounced man and wife, Dizzy pulled me into the tightest embrace and laid another praise-worthy kiss on me before we popped bottles of all types of liquor—taking full advantage of Loma's bar—and danced until our feet were sore and our nice wedding clothes were drenched in sweat. Since Loma had closed the club for the occasion, we celebrated late into the night. Dizzy and the band even gave us a little impromptu performance. He would take breaks between songs to pull me from my front row seat and twirl me around or to kiss me or to whisper something sweet or something naughty in my ear, then he'd return to the small stage and play his horn like only he could.

I smiled and laughed and giggled so much, I wondered if I was losing my mind. How could I be dead and be this totally, deliriously happy? How could I love this man, who was long gone from the world I'd come from, so much? How was it that my heart felt like it would burst with joy and passion for him? As I closed my eyes and let the music and cheering around me fill my ears, I decided to be thankful that in death, I'd found what I'd never known in life—love and true happiness.

When it seemed that everyone had partied themselves into exhaustion, Dizzy took my hand and led me up the stairs to my room. The boys in the band had agreed to double-up in the other rooms so that we could have some privacy on our wedding night. I had asked Dizzy why he didn't just rent us a room somewhere. He told me that he was saving his money to buy me a surprise. I was definitely okay with that.

Once we were inside the familiar walls of my room, Mr. Dizzy Gillespie undressed me slowly, as if he was enjoying the suspense of revealing my body to himself inch by inch. He took care rolling my silk stockings down each of my legs, drumming his fingers along my skin as if playing a tune on his trumpet. After he lifted my dress over my head, he gently smoothed my hair and sucked in a breath as he gazed at me. Once I was fully undressed, he stood and stared at me with a faint, satisfied smile on his face, as if my body was just what he'd expected or maybe even more. Then he kneeled before me and gently rubbed his hands up and down my bare thighs, pressed a soft kiss against my stomach. "My, my, my, J'Nay," he said. "*My... my... my.*"

My body trembled with excitement and anticipation. I held my breath as he stood, undressed himself, laid me in my bed, and went about the business of loving every single inch of me. It was almost as if he'd found a user's manual for my body and memorized it. Every touch, every single touch he gave me sent chills throughout my body, made me want to run away and stay at the same time. It had been years prior to my death since I'd been with a man, and even then, it wasn't anything to brag about. Actually, I had worked hard to forget about that lackluster rendezvous. But right at that moment, as Dizzy's lips gently brushed the small of my back, I knew that for the first time in my life, I was being made love to and when he was done making love to me, I made love to him.

Later that night, or should I say early the next morning,

when all was still and quiet around us, I settled in my new husband's arms and rested my head on his chest. "I love you, John 'Dizzy' Gillespie," I whispered.

And though I was sure he was asleep, he moved his head enough to plant a soft kiss on my forehead, and he said, "I love you, too, songbird."

Chapter Fifteen

"The Man I Love"

Esther served us breakfast in bed the next morning and once we finished eating, we stayed in that bed and got reacquainted with each other like we had the night before. By the time I emerged from that room, I felt a little dizzy in the head and I giggled softly to myself as I tip-toed to the bathroom. *I guess that's why they call him Dizzy,* I thought. I had heard of women losing their minds over certain men because of their bedroom skills and at that moment, I understood why. At that point, we could've made love every hour of every day for the rest of eternity and it wouldn't have bothered me a bit.

I relieved myself and then gathered some water and towels for me and Dizzy so that we could get dressed and face the world on our first official full day as man and wife. As I left the bathroom, Lila met me in the hall. She looked a little sad. As a matter of fact, she looked like she'd been crying.

"You okay, Lila?" I asked.

She looked up at me as if she hadn't noticed me before. She eyed me from head to toe. "You're glowing."

I smiled. "Thank you. Are you okay? What's wrong?"

She suddenly gave me a smirk. "You should try to be a little quieter tonight. We could *all* hear you, you know."

I felt blood rush to my cheeks. I opened my mouth to respond but couldn't think of anything to say. I didn't realize I'd been so loud. But if they knew what I knew, they would totally understand. Finally, I managed to say, "Uh... sorry about that."

"Mm-hmm. Harry was just here."

With raised eyebrows, I said, "Oh?"

She shook her head and laughed bitterly. "You really don't even care about him, do you? A good woman like me, he overlooks. Still pining away for *Junie*. He came 'round this morning wanting to know why Loma closed up the club last night. When Loma told him about you and Dizzy getting married, he broke down and cried like a baby."

I adjusted the heavy water jug in my hands. "Well, I'm sorry to hear that, but I don't love Harry. I thought the two of you—"

"Humph, I thought so, too," she said and then shrugged past me and went into Betty's room and slammed the door shut.

I stood there staring at the door for a minute, confused. Why was she so angry? Did she really care that much about Harry? A few days earlier, she was cozying up to that pianist. It just didn't make any sense. I tried to shake off the confusion as I headed back to my room. As soon as I saw my husband sitting on the side of the bed waiting for me, all thoughts of Lila and Harry fled from my mind. I placed the water on the dresser, soaked and squeezed out a small towel, and before I could begin washing him, he grabbed my hand and laid back on the bed, pulling me on top of him. When our mouths connected, I knew the water would be cold before we made use of it.

Later that evening, Dizzy left and I stayed in the room and tried not to feel so giddy, but how could I help feeling that way? I was married to a handsome, talented man and since we were already dead, I knew we'd never be apart. I'd heard people, preachers mostly, speak of the wonder and majesty of Heaven. I'd heard about the golden streets, the light, the angels, but all of that paled in comparison to what I was experiencing. The unmistakable true love that Dizzy and I shared was beautiful and rare and, I was convinced, only something that could exist in its purest form right here in Heaven. And I was so thankful that I was able to experience it. I just wished I could tell someone I knew how it felt. I mean, sure, I knew the folks here at the house, but they didn't know me. Not really. They knew Junie Walker. I longed to talk to someone who knew J'Nay Walker.

I sighed as I looked at my reflection in the mirror. There was no need in longing for the familiarity of the people from my former life. What I had, what I was living with Dizzy, was better than good—it was perfect, and it was all I needed. The dreams of my life were nice, but here, I was living with a music legend, loving him and being loved by him. It just didn't get any better than that.

♫

When Dizzy returned, he came upstairs and led me outside. He had me close my eyes before he opened the front door. He held my hand, led me outside, and when he directed me to open my eyes, I nearly fainted. Sitting in front of Loma's place was a shiny new Plymouth. It was creamy white and absolutely beautiful!

"When we leave here tomorrow, we gonna be riding in style. The other guys are gonna ride in the old car, so it'll just be me and you in this baby. You like it?"

I clamped my hand over my mouth and nodded before grabbing him and hugging him tightly. "Yes! I love it, John! It's beautiful."

He cradled my face in his hands and kissed me softly. "Not as beautiful as my songbird."

I smiled. "Thank you."

He returned my smile and then turned and trotted toward the car. "I almost forgot!"

He reached into the car through the open passenger window and pulled out a white box wrapped with a red satin bow. He walked back up the front steps and handed the box to me.

"For you, lovely."

I took the box and looked up at him with wide eyes. "Really? Thank you, John. Thank you so much."

He placed his hand on my back and led me into the house. "Come on, let's open it."

I followed him inside, up the stairs, and into our bedroom where I sat on the side of the bed and gently slid the beautiful ribbon off of the box. I gasped as I opened the box and lifted my gift up. I held it to my body and looked down at it as tears filled my eyes. "It's so lovely, John. It's so lovely."

"I want you to wear it to the club tonight."

I frowned. "It's a beautiful gown, John, but I can't work in it. It'll be ruined in no time flat."

Dizzy chuckled. "No, baby. You ain't working tonight. You gon' be sitting at the front table watching me and the boys play just for you."

"But... I can't let Loma down."

"Girl, this is your last night here and we got to get used to not having you, anyway. Listen to your husband. Any man worth a nickel wouldn't allow his wife to work around all them drunk-ass men no way," Loma said. I hadn't noticed her standing in the doorway.

I smiled as I stood from the bed and held the beautiful, red velvet scoop neck dress up to my body and admired it in the mirror.

"You are gonna look so pretty in that, Junie," Loma gushed.
I smiled at Dizzy. "Yes, I am."

CHAPTER SIXTEEN
"Blue Moon"

There was something magical about that night. I'm not sure if it was the dress—because it fit me to a tee. Or maybe it was the mellow crowd that poured into Loma's that night. Or perhaps it was the music, because it seemed that being married had given Dizzy's trumpet playing wings. He hopped and bebopped all over that stage, blasting notes—high and low— like there was no tomorrow. I sat at a table that grazed the dancefloor with my legs crossed, swaying and bouncing in my seat. My eyes never left Dizzy Gillespie, and his eyes never left me.

Halfway through the third song, Jessie pulled a chair to my table and sat next to me with a huge smile on her face. She leaned in close and said, "I'm so happy for you, Junie. You got yourself a good man, and you're leaving this place."

A light bulb went off in my head. "Hey, why don't you come with us? I'm sure Dizzy won't mind, but I'll ask him to be sure."

She gave me a warm smile and shook her head. "Everything's working out just fine for me." She turned and pointed out one of the back tables. There, dressed to the nines, was Dexter Toussard. "After I told him about the baby, he left his wife. Got us a place and everything," she gushed.

I glanced over at Dexter again, and then fixed my gaze on Jessie. "His wife is okay with this?"

She shook her head. "Naw, he said she didn't take it well, but he says everything's gonna be all right. Dexter says she ain't gon' do nothing."

I frowned deeply. "She's already done something, Jessie— throwing a brick through the window, busting up in here ranting and raving. There's no telling what she might do now."

She grasped my hand and smiled at me again. "I'm not worried. I trust Dexter. Everything is gonna be fine." She pulled me into a hug and I rubbed her back, closed my eyes, and said a quick prayer for her and her baby.

"Well, let me get back to work. I'm taking your place out here tonight."

"Thank you, Jessie."

She stood from the table, bent over and kissed me softly on the cheek, and then she left.

For the next couple of songs, my mind was in a fog, full of worry for Jessie. It wasn't until I heard my name, my *real* name being called, that I snapped out of it. I glanced around the room to see all eyes on me. Then I looked up and saw Dizzy staring at me. He smiled widely and nodded his head. I gave him a confused look. He approached the table and reached for my hand. I shook my head, still not sure what was going on.

He leaned in and whispered, "Come sing, songbird. I want the world to hear that voice." Then he kissed me lightly on the lips.

How in the world was I supposed to refuse a request that was sealed with a kiss? So I stood to my feet and whispered, "What am I supposed to sing?"

He grinned, flashing his dimples and making my heart flutter. "How about 'Summertime?'"

I nodded and let him lead me to the stage.

I nervously stood at the microphone and closed my eyes, unable to face the crowd of people whose eyes were all undoubtedly on me, giving me curious looks, wondering what in the world "Junie" was doing standing on that stage in that dress. As the band began to play the dramatic opening to the song, I took a deep breath, opened my mouth, and let my voice join them in performing the standard tune that I'd grown up listening to with my grandmother—*Loma*.

Midway through the first verse, I opened my eyes to find shocked and delighted looks on the faces of Loma's patrons. There were surprised smiles on the faces of the people I'd come to know as my friends—the people I shared a home with and worked with. I smiled, myself, as I continued to sing the song. And then a reality hit me. There I was, singing with the best of the best. I was singing with Dizzy Gillespie's band. In my former life, I had never, and probably would have never, experienced anything as special and grand as this. And to top it all off, I loved him and he loved me—and we were married. *We were married.*

As those thoughts played in my head, I felt a surge of emotion that served to bolster my voice. I suddenly felt the lyrics like never before. And when the song had ended, I bowed my head as the entire room erupted in applause and cheers. Dizzy, trumpet in hand, slid his arm around my waist, and with a huge grin on his face, planted a kiss on my cheek. The other band members patted him on the back as if congratulating him on *my* performance. Loma rushed to the small stage with Esther on her heels. They both grabbed me and hugged me and gushed about how they had no idea I could sing *like that*. I took it all in, realizing that I finally had what I had always dreamed of—fame. Maybe it wasn't on a national level. Maybe I wasn't a household name, but right then and there at Loma's place, I was every bit of a star as any other star in the galaxy.

I stood to the side of the stage and smiled and nodded and thanked person after person as Dizzy and his band began to play an up-tempo song. Couples began to crowd the dancefloor and Esther and Loma went back to selling liquor and cigarettes. Out of the corner of my eye, I could see Jessie at the table with her beau. *So much for her taking my place,* I thought. They were staring into each other's eyes, oblivious to what was going on around them. I doubt that they had heard even one of the notes I'd sung. As the small crowd of admirers surrounding me began to disperse, I noticed the front door slowly opening. My eyes widened as a disheveled-looking Katrina Toussard stumbled into the room, gun in hand. I opened my mouth to warn Jessie, but as I turned back to their table, I noticed Harry standing directly behind them. I hadn't even realized he was at the club. There he was, a wild look in his eyes... and a gun in *his* hand.

"Jessie! Look out!" I finally shouted. The music was too loud. No one heard me, least of all Jessie.

Panic-stricken, I climbed onto the small stage again and yelled into the microphone. "Jessie!"

The music stopped and all eyes were now on me. Dizzy moved next to me. "What is it?" he asked softly. "What is it, J'Nay?"

"Gun," I replied. "They both have a gun."

Murmurs filled the room as people turned from side to side, trying to figure out who "they" were. Dizzy's eyes followed mine. Katrina was still by the door with her gun at her side. Harry raised his gun, pointing at... at me? Dizzy?

"You can't leave me for her!" Katrina shouted. Somehow, she'd moved from the door to Jessie's table in a second flat. She pointed her gun at Jessie. Harry kept his gun trained on me and Dizzy. Then, a third gun… held in Lila's hand. Lila, who was standing right next to me, held her gun at my head. "Lila? Wh… why?"

She didn't answer me. She just cocked her gun. So did Harry and Katrina. They all cocked their guns at the same time. No one moved or even breathed. I cut my eyes at Dizzy. "I love you," I whispered.

"J'Nay! J'Nay!" Dizzy yelled over and over again, his voice becoming more and more hollow with each second that passed. "Songbird, I love you! I love you!"

And then three gunshots rang out at the same time… and everything went black.

Chapter Seventeen

"Good Morning Heartache"

"J'Nay… J'Nay. Wake up. Please, wake up..." The voice sounded like it was a millennium away. It was shaky, full of sorrow, and it belonged to Dizzy.

As my eyes fluttered open, and the blindingly bright light invaded my pupils, I wondered what had happened. Had I died again? Where was I now? In some other part of Heaven? And Dizzy. Was he okay?

"Dizzy," I whispered.

A face wearing a concerned look appeared before mine. "J'Nay? J'Nay, did you say something? Are you awake?"

It was him! It was my Dizzy, my John. But instead of his signature soul patch, jagged hair covered his jaws and chin.

I let my eyes focus on him. "John, you're okay?"

His mouth spread into a smile, and even through the coarse hair, I could see his dimples. "I'm fine. Are *you* okay? You scared us, J'Nay. I mean, you *really* scared us."

I smiled, my eyes half-open as my lids felt extremely heavy. And then I became keenly aware of a stabbing ache in the side of my head. I lifted my hand and touched my head, my fingers grazing a coarse bandage. "My head hurts."

Dizzy chuckled lightly. "I'd imagine so."

I frowned slightly at his words, his voice. Something was different about him but I couldn't readily put my finger on it. "John... John, I love you," I whispered.

I watched as his brow furrowed deeply. "You do?" he asked, surprise evident in his voice.

Something definitely wasn't right. I forced my eyelids to retreat completely, allowing me a full, somewhat fuzzy view of my surroundings. There was a TV, machines beeping, fluorescent lights. "Where... where am I?"

"You're in the hospital, J'Nay. You were shot. Do you remember?"

I stared at him and the realization of what was going on finally hit me. I was alive. It was 2015 again. And this was John Folks at my bedside—*not* Dizzy Gillespie. My Dizzy, my John, was gone. And I hadn't saved Jessie. Before I could stop myself, I broke down in racking sobs. John—John Folks placed his hand on my shoulder and whispered reassuring words to me, but nothing he said made me feel any better. My heart, my happiness was gone. I was alive, and for the first time in my life, I wished I was dead. I wished more than anything that I was in Heaven again.

I cried uncontrollably for hours, feeling a mixture of marked relief at the fact that I wasn't dead and deep sorrow at the thought of never seeing or loving Dizzy again. The nurses kept asking me if I was in pain, did I remember what happened to me. I could only shake my head and cry harder. Poor John didn't have a clue as to what to do. Every time my tears would slow up enough for me to get a glimpse of him, he would be sitting in the corner with a bewildered and confused look on his face.

I cried throughout the doctor's gentle physical examination of me. I cried when John finally left. I cried when they brought me my dinner. I cried so hysterically that they eventually gave me a sedative. And as the skies outside my window began to darken, I cried myself to sleep. All the while, Loma's words played over and over in my head:

"He's just passing through. Ain't nothing ahead for you but heartache if you start up with him."

She was partially right. My heart was aching, but I had been the one who was just passing through.

♫

The next morning, my heart was still heavy, but I didn't cry. My head throbbed and my vision was blurred. My mouth was stuck together, and after lying there trying to figure out what was wrong with me, I realized it was the sedative. It had calmed me, but the after effects were horrible. I squinted my eyes in the harsh overhead lighting and reached for the button on the bed to raise my head. As my fingers clumsily searched for the button, I heard movement from across the room. My eyes drifted to where the noise had come from to see John Folks rising from an uncomfortable-looking chair, making his way toward me.

He gave me an uncertain smile and said, "Good morning."

I shifted my eyes back to the railing, searching for the button. "Morning," I said. *There's nothing good about anything anymore,* I thought.

"What are you trying to do?" he asked. "Let me help you."

I shook my head as my finger finally landed on the button. I raised the head of the bed and felt a little woozy. I closed my eyes.

"I need to use the bathroom," I said softly.

"Okay, let me go tell the nurse."

The nurse not only helped me walk to the toilet on my rubbery legs, she also helped me shower and put on a clean gown. While leaning against the face bowl, brushing my teeth, I caught a glimpse of my swollen face and shaved head, half of which was covered with a white bandage. I shuddered at my appearance. I looked like I'd just survived a war or something.

The nurse helped me back into my bed, and as she left, I pulled the covers over my legs and noticed that John was still in the room. He was sitting in the corner, staring at me.

I closed my eyes and sighed. "Why are you here?" I asked.

"What?"

I opened my eyes and fixed them on John, whose likeness to my Dizzy nearly sent me into a torrent of tears again. "Why are you here?" I repeated.

"Because you asked for me."

I frowned slightly, rubbed my throbbing head, felt the bandage covering the side of it. "What are you talking about?"

He moved closer to the bed and twisted his mouth to one side, revealing a single dimple. I blinked back tears. "Do you remember anything, J'Nay? Anything at all about the shooting, your aunt?"

I nodded slightly. "I remember that she was shot, and I think I was, too."

He nodded. "You were. Do you remember when it happened? I mean, do you know what day it is now?"

I shook my head. "No, I don't."

He leaned in closer. "That was a month ago, J'Nay."

"A month? I've been in the hospital for a month?"

He nodded.

"What... I don't remember being in here that long."

"That's because you were in a coma. Yesterday was the first time you opened your eyes."

I rubbed my forehead. "Then I'm confused. How could I have asked for you if I was in a coma?"

He shrugged. "I don't know. But you did. You said my name over and over again... unless you know another John."

I just stared at him. There was no way I could explain the other John I knew without sounding like a nutcase.

"Your cousin, Linda, was here with you the first time you said my name. When she told me, I knew I had to be here with you. I've been coming to see you, to sit with you and talk to you, every day for the last three weeks. I even played music for you." He smiled and pointed to a small boom box sitting in the corner of the room, next to the chair he'd vacated. "I'm so glad you woke up."

I nodded slightly, tore my eyes away from his lit-up face. I reached up and rubbed the bandage on my head. "I was shot in the head?"

He nodded. "There was a little brain damage. The doctors are surprised you woke up. They didn't give you much of a chance of making it, J'Nay. But I prayed for you. I prayed so hard." His eyes clouded a bit and he turned his head.

I continued to finger the bandage. "Brain damage?"

He turned his face to me again. "Yes. The doctor said he'd come in and talk to you about it later today if you're calm enough."

I nodded and closed my eyes. I heard John move, and when I opened my eyes again, he was back in his seat in the corner of the room.

"How is my aunt?" I asked.

John stood from the chair and was back at my bedside in

seconds. He rested his hand on top of mine. "She didn't make it, J'Nay. They've already had her funeral. Linda and Ronnie didn't want to wait since they weren't sure you'd make it."

I nodded as a single tear escaped my eye. "Was anyone else shot?"

John shook his head. "One of the customers, a guy, tackled the man with the gun after he shot you. The guy who shot you is in jail now."

I fixed my eyes on John's face. "Who was he? Why did he do it? Was it a robbery?"

John leaned against the bed railing. "No, he's mentally disturbed—schizophrenic. Said the voices told him to do it."

I blew out a frustrated sigh. "I see, so probably nothing's gonna happen to him. Just a few months in the loony bin, and then he'll be free to hurt or kill someone else."

"I pray that's not the case, J'Nay. I pray that justice is served."

At that moment, I didn't want to hear a thing about prayer or anything of the sort. A cruel trick had been played on me. Evidently, in my comatose state, I had dreamt the whole 1939 scene up. But the dream had been so real and vivid. And how was it possible to feel the emotions I felt during a dream? How could I have fallen in love? How could I still be in love? None of it made any sense, and it frustrated the hell out of me that I couldn't understand it.

"J'Nay, you said you loved me on yesterday." John's soft, uncertain voice snatched me from my thoughts.

"I know."

"Did you… did you mean it?"

I stared at him for a moment and decided to tell him the truth. "At that moment, I think I did, John." *Or at least I loved the John I thought you were.*

A smile played at the corners of his mouth. "I'm glad to hear that. Um, I told you this a bunch of times when you were in that coma, but I need to tell you now that I lo—"

The doctor burst into the room, interrupting us. As the doctor pulled a chair to my bedside, I saw John duck out of the room from the corner of my eye.

The doctor told me that the bullet had affected the part of the brain that controls emotions. He said that was why I couldn't stop crying the day before. He said I would have trouble controlling my emotions for the rest of my life, probably. I nodded and listened and tried to focus on what he was saying, but all I could think about was Dizzy Gillespie and the life I would never have with him. When the doctor was finished, he said, "Do you have any questions?"

I hesitated, and then said, "Yes, I do."

"Okay, go ahead."

"I… I had this dream when I was in the coma. It was so real…" the tears flooded my eyes and spilled over before I could stop them.

The doctor nodded sympathetically. "Some coma patients report having nightmares while in a coma."

I shook my head. "No, it wasn't a nightmare. It was the most beautiful dream I've ever had in my life. I wish… I wish it had been real. I thought it *was* real."

He leaned forward. "Remember what I said about your emotions now? It makes sense that you felt whatever happened in that dream very deeply. Your emotions were heightened. And I'm afraid that they will be from now on. But with some pharmaceutical treatment and the support of your family and friends, I think things will be manageable for you."

I sighed as I wiped my moist eyes. "I hope so."

CHAPTER EIGHTEEN

"They Can't Take That Away From Me"

The next day was another crying day for me. I was in tears from the moment I woke up, until the moment they sedated me and I drifted off to sleep. The day after that, I was angry for hours. Both days, despite my state, John Folks never left my side. No matter how hard I cried or what I threw at him, or how loudly I yelled, he stayed with me until visiting hours were over. I'd known he had a thing for me before all of this, but his level of dedication was mind-boggling. Why was he doing this? Was it because I said his name while I was in the coma or because I told him I loved him? If so, he deserved to know the full truth. Both of those things had been about Dizzy—not him.

The day I decided to confess the truth to John, he didn't show up. Instead, my cousins, Ronnie and Linda, who I had come to know as Harry and Lila, came to visit me along with some of the other workers from the restaurant. We all talked and reminisced about Aunt Iris—how she could be demanding one minute and nurturing the next. We shared some laughs and some tears. And when they left, I found myself feeling lonely and empty. It took hours for me to come to the realization that I missed John Folks' company. He wasn't much for words when he was around, but his presence was familiar and comforting, and I guess he had grown on me in some ways. Evidently, I'd come to rely on his presence.

That evening, Dab came by to see me. He told me about several projects he had lined up for me. "Hurry up and get better," he teased. I should've been excited about the news he gave me. My singing career was everything to me, right? But it wasn't. At least not anymore. After all, I had shared a stage with *the* Dizzy Gillespie. It just doesn't get any better than that. Besides, I wasn't even sure if I could still sing at all. I also wasn't sure if I *wanted* to sing anymore.

After Dab left, I lay in my bed, staring at the ceiling, thinking about my life and the dream that had rocked my world and broken my heart. What the doctor had said made perfect sense, but there was still a part of me that had trouble believing that what I'd experienced was just a dream. I could still smell the liquor and cigarette smoke in Loma's club. I could still hear Dizzy's trumpet filling my ears. I could still feel the pads of Dizzy's fingertips as he caressed me.

I took a deep breath and began to softly sing "Summertime," and I could hear for myself that my voice was intact. Tears filled my eyes as I stopped the song after the first verse.

"Excuse me," came a voice from out of nowhere.

I frowned slightly as I turned my head and peered through

the room that had been darkened by nightfall. "Yes?"

The light over my bed flickered on and I could see a petite young woman standing by the door. Her hand was gripping the pole of an electronic vital sign machine. She eased into the room cautiously, her large, round eyes fixed on me. "My name is Freda. I'm your nurse aide for tonight and I need to check your vital signs."

I nodded, closed my eyes, and turned my head.

I could hear the wheels of the monitor squeak as she moved closer to the bed. "That was beautiful—your singing, I mean."

With my eyes still closed, I said, "Thank you."

"You feeling okay, tonight?" she asked.

Her voice seemed oddly familiar for some reason. I opened my eyes and glued them to her face as she wrapped the blood pressure cuff around my arm. She looked up at me and smiled. And that's when I realized where I knew her from. I lifted my head. "Betty?"

She frowned and looked at me. "No, Freda, remember?"

I blinked. "Oh, yeah. Sorry."

"That was my grandmother's name, though. She passed years ago."

"Was she from Louisiana?"

She slowly nodded.

I rested my head against the back of the bed. "I knew her once, a long time ago."

She cocked her head to the side. "You did? You from Louisiana?"

I nodded. "She was so sweet when she was younger. And tiny, like you."

Freda smiled. "She was sweet until the day she died. And everyone always says I look just like her."

"You do."

Freda removed the cuff from my arm. "So, how well did you know her?"

"Pretty well. We used to… work together."

Her brow furrowed deeply. "Really? Where?"

"Uh… at a little night spot in New Orleans. It closed down a long time ago."

"Hmm, I'll have to ask my mama what you're talking about. Only night spot I ever heard Grandma Betty talk about was Loma's. But that was way back in the 30s or 40s or something. Way before your time. But Grandma Betty was something else. She was still going to blues festivals when she was up in her eighties. Ain't no telling about her."

I smiled nervously.

"Well, it was good to meet you…" She consulted the chart in her hands and added, "Ms. Walker."

"Good to meet you, too."

After she left, I smiled until I finally fell asleep. I knew that dream was real.

♫

The realization that the dream was real sent me into a deep depression. For days, I didn't eat. I couldn't sleep. I was so miserable, I couldn't even cry. I just lay in that bed with my eyes focused on a spot on the wall. I was too hurt to feel anything. I'm not sure how that's even possible, but it was the truth.

And every day, good old faithful John Folks never left my side. Sometimes, he would tell me about what was going on with the restaurant as Linda and Ronnie worked hard to keep it open to honor their mother and our grandmother. Sometimes he would play music for me—jazz standards. And sometimes he would just sit there in silence. At times, I would let my eyes drift to his face and I would let his likeness to Dizzy transport me back to Loma's, to my bedroom, to Dizzy's love. Other times, I would avoid his face altogether.

This went on for more than a week. Then the doctor announced that there was no physical reason for me to stay in the hospital. There was nothing more they could do for me because I was healed. The only options were transfer to a mental health facility, or I could go home and see a psychiatrist on an outpatient basis. My cousins, who were my next of kin, took me home to Loma's Soul Food. And there, in my bed, in a room that was a replica of the one I'd shared with Dizzy, I sank deeper into my depression.

Chapter Nineteen

"Love Walked In"

I lay there with a heavy, aching heart beating in rhythm with my sorrow. My eyes were closed, but I wasn't asleep. Sleep had absconded hours earlier, leaving me lying there with my misery and grief.

I sighed and silently said the only prayer I could manage at the moment. "Lord, send me back. Please, send me back to him. I miss him so much."

Out of the blue, Sarah Vaughan's version of "You Go to My Head" began to play, followed by a voice saying, "Get up, J'Nay. Rise and shine!"

Startled, I rolled over in bed with a frown on my face. Standing in my bedroom, opening the curtains, was John Folks. His cell phone was providing the music.

"Get out," I grunted.

"You *can* talk. Linda and Ronnie told me you couldn't."

I raised up on my elbows and wondered what his deal was. I'd never heard him speak so loudly before. "I *don't* talk, not *can't*. There's a difference. Turn that music off."

He turned the volume down a little instead of turning the song off. "I bet you can eat, too. They told me you haven't been doing that, either."

I sighed and collapsed back onto the bed. "Look, I appreciate you for being there for me while I was in the hospital; I really do. But I'm not in the mood for this today, and you're gonna make me mad. And you know if I get mad I can't control it."

He folded his arms across his chest and shook his head. "You can't claim that, J'Nay. Just because the doctor said it, doesn't make it law. He also said you were gonna die."

"I wish I had," I mumbled.

He wore a look of deep concern. "Why?"

I rolled over and faced the wall. "You wouldn't understand."

"How do you know? Try me."

Salty tears rushed from my eyes, dampening the covers beneath my head. "I lost something that meant a lot to me, someone I loved very, very much. Nothing else matters now."

"We all lost someone we loved."

I knew he thought I was referring to Aunt Iris. "I'm not just talking about my aunt, John. I'm talking about someone else."

"Who, J'Nay?"

I felt him sit on the side of the bed. I rolled over and faced him. "If I tell you something, will you promise not to think I'm crazy?" I really wanted to tell someone about the dream, about Loma's and everyone I'd grown to know and love there. No, I *needed* to tell someone.

He slowly nodded. "I could never think you were crazy, J'Nay."

I scooted up in the bed and rested my back against the headboard. I took a deep breath, released it, and told him everything. I told him about Dizzy, about how much I loved him, about how badly I missed him. He never took his eyes off of me as I spoke. He seemed to be absorbing my every word.

"So there it is. Dizzy was the John I was referring to. I'm so sorry," I said in conclusion.

John turned his head and fixed his eyes on the floor for a moment. Then he refocused on me with a thoughtful look on his face. "So you say Dizzy looked like me?"

"*Exactly* like you. Same dimples and everything. He wore glasses, too. Only difference is he had a little soul patch."

"Okay, can I tell you what I think the dream was about, what it meant?"

I nodded as he stood from the bed and began to pace my bedroom floor.

"I think he looked like me and you fell in love with him because you have feelings for me. I felt it that night at the piano. I felt a connection with you. I think you felt it, too. And I think you carried the feeling of that connection into your experience with the dream."

"But… I don't really believe it was a dream. Betty actually existed. I met her granddaughter."

"Could your grandmother have told you about her? Described her to you? Linda said you and her were really close when you were growing up. She said you spent a lot of time with her."

I sighed, realizing that he was probably right about Betty, and maybe even about Dizzy. "But the love he gave me felt so real... and his music..."

John reclaimed his seat on my bed and grasped my hand. He smiled, giving me a full view of both dimples. "Well, I played a fair share of his music for you when you were in the coma. His and other artists' music. And maybe his love felt real because I love you, J'Nay. I've loved you for a long, long time. I did everything I could to make you feel my love when you were in that coma."

My eyes widened. I knew he liked me, but *love*? "What? You... you *love* me?"

"Yes, *I love you*. Just always been too shy to tell you. But when I almost lost you, I prayed and made a promise to God that if He saved you, I wouldn't waste another second being shy. I'm not wasting precious time anymore, watching you from afar, wanting you and doing nothing to have you. So here's the bold, new me. You think it was Dizzy's love you felt, but it was mine. It was my love willing you to come back to me, and you did, thanks to God. *You did*." He leaned in close to me and gently brushed my lips with his, and sparks shot through me. He softly rubbed his hand across the short, fine hair on my head.

After he ended the kiss, my eyes popped open, and I looked at him. I mean, I *really* looked at him, and for the first time, I saw more than the shy cook with the nice smile and gentle voice. I saw John—*my* John.

"Now, the way I see it, you can keep pining away for your Dizzy, or you can open your eyes and see that he's right in front of you. You can either keep wishing for his love, or you can accept mine," he said as he softly rubbed the back of his hand along my cheekbone.

I stared at him for a moment, and then I smiled. His words, the cadence of his voice, his smile, his eyes—I finally saw it. I finally saw what I'd been missing for so long. I had thought that John resembled Dizzy. But all the while, Dizzy resembled John. John Folks had prayed for me, stayed by my side, and talked to me while I was comatose, and, according to him, had loved me for a long time though I was oblivious to the fact. Yes, *this* was my John.

It was at that moment that I realized the purpose of me being shot and falling into a coma and having that dream. Before, all I thought about was being a success. Now, all I cared about was living and loving and being loved. Now, I knew that the most important thing in this life was what I had found in 1939.

"What's it gonna be?" he asked, standing from the bed. "You need me to grow a soul patch, because I'll do it."

I shook my head. "You don't need a soul patch. I just opened my eyes, and I see you, John. I really see you. I wanna accept what you have to give me. I wanna accept your love."

He grinned. "*Finally!*" He reached for my hand. "Will you come downstairs and have breakfast with me? I cooked."

I took his hand and slowly stood to my feet. "Isn't that your job, to cook?"

He pulled me into his arms and kissed me. "My job is to love you, lovely."

I leaned against him and sighed. "Well, I guess my job is to love you, too, John Folks. Because if it was your love I felt when I was in that coma, then all of the love I have to give is for you. I love you, too."

He kissed me again. "Good."

"Will you play the piano for me?"

"I sure will. But only if you'll sing for me, songbird."

"Okay, but my voice isn't at its best right now. I'm a little out of practice."

"I know it's gonna be beautiful like always."

We stood there in each other's arms in the middle of my bedroom floor for a moment before John finally released me and said, "Let me grab your robe for you. There are some customers down there, but I'm taking you to the private dining room."

I nodded and then realized what he'd just said. My heart skipped a beat. "You called me 'lovely' and 'songbird.'"

He pulled my robe from my closet and helped me into it. "Yes, because you *are* lovely and you *are* a songbird."

I looked him in the eye. "But you've never called me those names before."

"Sure I have, J'Nay. Sure I have." He gave me a wink, flashed me a dimpled grin, and grasped my hand, leading me to the dining room.

If you enjoyed *Summertime*, please consider leaving a review on the website of your choice.

Please support The Jazz Education Network by visiting:

http://www.jazzednet.org/

Please also consider supporting the Jazz Foundation of America which is dedicated to saving the homes and lives of elder jazz and blues musicians in crisis:

http://jazzfoundation.org/about-jazz-foundation-america

For more information about Adrienne Thompson, visit:

http://adriennethompsonwrites.webs.com

Sign up for Adrienne's newsletter here:

http://eepurl.com/jnDmH

Follow Adrienne on Twitter!

https://twitter.com/A_H_Thompson

Like Adrienne on Facebook!

https://www.facebook.com/AdrienneThompsonWrites

Follow Adrienne on Pinterest!

http://www.pinterest.com/ahthompsn/

Also by Adrienne Thompson

The *Bluesday* Series:
Bluesday
Lovely Blues
Blues In The Key Of B
Locked out of Heaven (Tomeka's Story – A Bluesday Continuation)

The *Been So Long* Series:
Rapture (A Been So Long Prequel)
If (Wasif's Story) A Been So Long Prequel
Been So Long
Little Sister (Cleo's Story—a companion novel to Been So Long)
Been So Long 2 (Body and Soul)
Been So Long III (Whatever It Takes)

The *Your Love Is King* Series
Your Love Is King
Better

Stand-alone novels:
Home
Ain't Nobody
See Me
When You've Been Blessed (Feels Like Heaven)

Nonfiction Titles:
Just Between Us (Inspiring Stories by Women) –as a contributor
Seven Days of Change (A Flash Devotional)

All books are available at amazon.com, barnesandnoble.com, and kobobooks.com

"So, you think maybe you could give me your number?"

"My number?"

He nodded and clasped his hands together. "Pretty please?"

I tried not to smile. "Well, what if I told you I already have a man and that he's back home waiting for me and he doesn't like me giving my phone number out to other guys?"

"Then I'd say that what he doesn't like doesn't matter to me since he was fool enough to let you come all the way to St. Louis without him."

"Really, now?" I said with a raised eyebrow.

"*Really*. And I'd also say that it is my privilege and my duty to take you off his hands."

"Off his hands? You make me sound like I'm some unattended land or something."

"I meant to make you sound like an unguarded treasure."

I rolled my eyes. "Mm-hmm."

"Do you?"

"Do I what?"

"Have a man?"

"No, I don't. Do you have a woman?"

"That depends on whether or not you give me your number."

"That's not an answer."

"No, I don't... *yet*."

I smiled despite myself. "Yet?"

"*Yet*. Now, may I please have your number?"

I sighed. "Okay, but if I give you my number, it doesn't mean we're anything more than friends."

He leaned in until his lips nearly touched mine, looked me dead in the eye, and said, "Then I'll just have to take what I can get until I can change your mind."

www.ingramcontent.com/pod-product-compliance
Lightning Source LLC
Chambersburg PA
CBHW051306250626
47155CB00009B/3455